LILLIAN SIMMONS

OR

THE CONFLICT OF SECTIONS

AMS PRESS

NEW YORK

LILLIAN SIMMONS

OR

THE CONFLICT OF SECTIONS

A STORY BY

OTIS M. SHACKELFORD, A. B.

Author of "A Dream of Freedom Realized," "Seeking
the Best," and Other Essays and Poems

SECOND EDITION

Illustrated by

William Hamilton

Press of
R. M. RIGBY PRINTING CO.
Kansas City

Library of Congress Cataloging in Publication Data

Shackelford, Otis M.   1871-
   Lillian Simmons: or, The conflict of sections.

   Reprint of the 2d ed. printed by R. M. Rigby
Print. Co., Kansas City, Mo.
   I. Title.
PZ3.S5228Li7   [PS3537.H12]   813'.4   73-18607
ISBN 0-404-11417-2

Reprinted from an original copy in the collections of
the Indiana University Library.

From the edition of 1915, Kansas City, Missouri, Second edition
First AMS edition published in 1975
Manufactured in the United States of America

AMS PRESS INC.
NEW YORK, N.Y. 10003

To a departed father, to a beloved mother, to devoted sisters and brothers; is this volume lovingly dedicated by,

THE AUTHOR.

PREFACE

In our travels, North and South, we find among our people certain social evils and false notions of life, which need to be corrected. Unity of action, and of opinion, in all sections of this country, is absolutely necessary, if we would progress in social and business uplift. And in order to call attention to many of our short comings and things which tend to stint our growth, as a race, or nation, we write this story of "Lillian Simmons" or "The Conflict of Sections."

It is based upon some of the vital questions and problems of the day.

It is a love story which creates interest and claims the attention, and at the same time touches upon the various phases of the race problem in a pleasing yet subtle way. Separate schools, the "Jim Crow Car," segregation in its many forms, and other things pertaining to the welfare of the race, are discussed in turn.

Our characters are clear cut, and are portrayed in an intensely human way, representing types not only of our own colored

race, but they are typical of the entire human
family. They are true to life. And we would
be happy could their names live forever.

But for this we do not hope. We do hope,
however, to inspire others of our race who are
literarily inclined, and to show forth the
great possibilities in this new field of en-
deavor. We as a race want a place in Literature. We want to be heroes in song and
story. We want to play leading roles on the
stage and in book. We want to stir the emotions of men. We want to provoke laughter,
tears and applause. We are tired of playing
the foolish, silly, insignificant part as given
to us by the literature of other races. And we
think the time has come for us to take this
line of work in hand.

The soil of the Negro literary field is indeed rich and abounds in vast tracts, from
which material for history, song, and story
may be gathered.

We hope this effort will inspire the boys
and girls of our race, who are being turned
out of our High Schools and Colleges each
year, and who have literary taste and inclina-
tion, to write along various lines. We would
ask them to use the grammar, the rhetoric,
and the correct English which they have
mastered, in the making of a literature and a

history for their race, in creating characters and heroes, that will live long after they are dead.

Take the stories from the lips of the old grandfathers and mothers, and with the skill which many of the young people possess, polish them up.

They will make interesting reading and in a few years from now, when the lips of the old are forever sealed, and the chance for obtaining much authentic history is forever gone, they will be of great value.

We hope that much good will come from our effort. We invoke the good will and sympathy of our readers. May our purpose inspire and please them if the story does not.

We wish to thank the Burton Publishing Company for suggestions and favors shown, and the good will that it has always extended to us. We highly recommend them to others who may have work like this to be done.

We also wish to thank Mr. William Hamilton, one of Missouri's best colored artists for illustrations. With his talent there is much good that he can do for his race.

And last, but by no means least, we wish to thank Mrs. Eva L. Lewis, of Paducah, Ky., for copying our manuscript in so beautiful a hand and preparing it for the press.

The parts that these people have played in producing "Lillian Simmons," or "The Conflict of Sections" are indispensable, and again we thank them.

With this we give the book into the hands of the Public. Let them use it as they will.

THE AUTHOR.

TABLE OF CONTENTS

LIST OF ILLUSTRATIONS

CHAPTER I

The North Against The South

Charles Christopher, a young colored man of the South, after having been knocked and tossed about in various ways, found himself many miles from home among strange people with strange ways and strange environments. The country contrasted with his own in many ways. Physical conditions were different—as were the customs and manners and brogue in speech. Hence for a long time he was at sea. He had lost his bearings as it were.

Having, however, found employment in a Northern hotel, for it was in the North he was now located, he was thrown in company with young men whose training was different to his, and which was in keeping with the section in which they lived.

He readily became acquainted with them and soon they were on very friendly and familiar terms. He did not know though how to take their jokes and slurs cast at him and the sunny country in which he lived and loved.

They were thoughtless young men, and knew not how deeply they were piercing the

heart of their new comrade with their satire.
They did not know that Charles Christopher,
though balked and checked by poverty, had a
fine sensitive nature; that his thoughts were
pure and his ideals were lofty; that he had a
high aim in life; that it was this high aim
which had led him on step by step until he
had completed his education in one of the
Southern ·Colleges.

Not one of his companions was equal to
him in book lore. But they were ignorant of
his preparation in many ways, for a great
and useful life. They felt themselves superior to him because they were born and raised
in the North. This argument alone they
thought sufficient to establish their superior-
ity. And to tell the truth this was the only
argument they had in their favor when com-
pared with Charles Christopher.

One morning after hours he went down
by the river side, as was a habit of his, to
watch the distant boats and water craft as
they plied to and fro and up and down stream.
While thus engaged his attention was attracted by loud and angry voices not far from
him. He arose and walked leisurely in the
direction of the seeming quarrel.

"You Southern niggers come up here and
spoil our privileges," were the words he distinctly heard as he approached. "There was

a time when we could eat in any restaurant in town and now we are barred from all down town places except Jim Allen's. We used to sit where we pleased in the theatres; we used to be permitted to go to any of the Parks, and now that's all over. Just because you Southern people have come up here with your ignorance and roughness. Why, I have taken my company many a time to the "Grand," and sat in the box on the first floor. I can't do it now."

At this juncture Charles approached the bunch of young men and calmly asked in what way had the Southern negroes spoiled their privileges.

"Why hello Charles," said the speaker who so passionately held the "floor." "Where did you spring from? I suppose you are here to champion the cause of the Southern darkies," said he sarcastically. "Well we are pretty good friends Charlie, but you are from the South and I must tell you the truth."

The speaker above mentioned and who seemed to be the leader in the harangue, was George Simmons, whose father was in fair circumstances, having served several years as clerk in the City Treasurer's office, and who, in his life time, had received good salaries at various other employments. He owned his own home which was very beautiful and well

kept and located in the very best part of the
city. His family consisted of his wife and
two children. George, who was now twenty-
two years of age, and his daughter Lillian,
now blooming into womanhood at eighteen.

Both children had finished in the High
School. Both had received honors at the close
of their school career and were well known
in the city, especialy among the school people.
George boasted of having "starred" on the
Foot Ball team, and Lillian had played substi-
tute on the Basket Ball team. Their records
for scholarship were good and they were very
popular.

And it was George with his many accomplishments, with his record in the High
School and his knowledge of existing previous
conditions, who now confronted Charles
Christopher, worked up to a high pitch of
excitement, and prepared to tell him the
plain truth.

George Simmons was a handsome youth
of medium build, graceful and athletic in his
movements. He was what might be called a
light brown skin in complexion, and had dark
hair, not of the finest grade which nature
gives to many colored people, neither was it
of the coarser kind, but it was such as was
very becoming to his complexion. He also
had an air of freedom and independence

about him which is usually in evidence with Northern born and Northern educated colored people. His training and high spirit showed perceptibly when he spoke with flashing eye to Charles Christopher.

"In what way have they spoiled our privileges? Why I can mention a dozen instances. Five years ago old Josh Greene came up here from the South, and the first week he was here he got smart. He went down to the park and sat down at one of the refreshment tables, and because one of the white waitresses was a little slow about waiting on him he became insolent, declaring that he was in there first, that his money was as good as anybodys, that he was not in the South now, and that he must be served at once. He raised so much Cain that they did serve him, but declared he would be the last colored person served in that place.

"And since that time no one of our race has been served there. Same thing happened when Pete Williams got in a fight with the manager of the boat house. He went out in a boat and stayed over time and did not want to pay. When he returned the manager demanded pay for over time. His reply was, "If you get pay out of me, you will have to take it out of my hide," whereupon the manager went after him and an awful fight ensued, in which the owner of the boat house was fearfully cut. The result was that all negroes were barred from the privileges of the park. Two years ago a drunken Negro from the South was sitting in the parquet of the Temple Theatre and raised a disturbance, yelling and applauding at the wrong time. He didn't know how to appreciate a good play. He laughed outright during a death-bed scene, and when an usher called him down he got sore and wanted to fight. After that the colored people had to sit in the gallery to themselves in the Temple Theatre and it was not long before the other theatres followed the Temple's example.

"And then you ask in what way have the Southern niggers spoiled our privileges. If I had my way I would have a law passed prohibiting this obnoxious influx from the South."

At this point in George Simmons' passionate speech Charles Christopher interrupted:

"You Northern people have yet to learn this lesson, George Simmons, that white people are white people, that blood is thicker than water, that the racial instinct will assert itself. That one bad negro cannot spoil the privileges of a community of good negroes, unless the prejudice in the hearts of the other race is aroused. They seek the slightest excuse for humiliating and imposing hardships upon our people. Why not seize these disturbers by the nape of the neck and the seat of the pants and hurl them bodily through the gates and doors of their places of amusements, thus making an example of such offenders for all time to come? This would be the proper way to proceed. This is what they do to their own offenders, and this would show respect for deserving, well-trained individuals of all races. Why bar the good on account of the bad. Why cast them all on a heap together and treat them all as unworthy? Tell me why, George Simmons, in a straight-forward, candid manner the reason why? Or have you ever tried to figure it out?"

At this juncture Charles paused for a reply. "There is but one reply George, if you are honest enough to make it, or if you have sense enough to see it. It is simply this: that prejudice is rapidly growing all over this country. It is taking or has taken deep root in your city. This is inevitable and it would have come sooner or later regardless of the conduct of these so-styled bad Southern "niggers." Like the wolf that wanted to devour the innocent lamb and for an excuse charged it with having muddled up his water in the stream where he was to drink. The lamb begged pardon and showed him where it was impossible for him to muddy up his drinking water since he was several yards below where he, the wolf, had to drink. The wolf could find no legal excuse for devouring the innocent lamb, so he pounced upon it without an excuse. So, through prejudice with or without an excuse, these harships are inflicted upon you."

"Oh no, you can't tell me that," said George Simmons impatiently. "For instance in the High School, colored boys have always played on the Foot Ball team and the Base Ball team. Colored girls have always played right along by the side of white girls on the Basket Ball team. I was 'Class Orator' of my class. Frank Mack was Valedictorian of his class. Each year honors have been distributed according to the merits of individual scholars, regardless of race, color or previous conditions. We have attended balls and parties given by white people here. And I am convinced of this fact that, wherever this rough, ignorant and uncouth class of Negroes can be controlled or held at bay, the whites of this section are fair and will exhibit no prejudice! My father has been clerk for ten years—And I don't care to discuss this subject with you any further. You had better carry your Southern ideas and prejudices out of this town. We don't need you to teach us any lessons. And my advice to you is to 'beat it.' There is always some stray Negro coming here advocating separate schools, Negro business, Negro this and that, scattering seeds of prejudice where no prejudice exists. And I am going to take it as a part of my duty to stop it. So you 'beat it' out of this town as soon as you can arrange to do so."

Charles Christopher was surprised at George's last utterance with its "background of passion," to use a President Wilson expression, but he was not nonplused by this argument. He knew that it was fallacious and he was prepared to overthrow it if George, through angry passion, had not brought the discussion to an abrupt close by an intentional insult. The thrust was more than his manhood could stand.

"What do you mean George Simmons?" His large eyes fairly gleaming with rage. "You know not what you say. Don't you know I had rather obey the call of death a hundred times than submit to your demand? I have no interest in this place, but I shall not leave until it pleases me to do so. As to this insult that you have directed with unerring aim at me, I shall not stand it. You must whip me right now for I am going to fight you with all the strength that is in my body. So prepare."

At this he began taking off his coat. By this time quite a crowd of loafers, white and colored had gathered, and were eager to see what promised to be a good fight, the young men being evenly matched in size, strength and skill. And too, each had friends or sympathizers in the crowd as was evidenced by the applause and encouragement that each received.

In less time than it takes to relate it, the young men were standing before each other, hatless and coatless, in true pugilistic attitude, seeking an opportunity to land a telling blow.

Seeking an opportunity to land a telling blow.

CHAPTER II

LILLIAN SIMMONS

Lillian Simmons was a beautiful brown skin maid of eighteen summers. And this particular morning as she stood on the front veranda of her father's stately home, with eyes that sparkled and black wavy hair that glistened in the sunlight, falling in a thick cluster of curls about her girlish neck, she looked more like the nymphs or fairies of the woods than she did the ordinary mortal at home.

Lillian, it must be admitted, was beautiful to an extraordinary degree, but she was not spoiled. She was handled and tutored by a very sensible mother who, though she loved her children, knew too much about them to spoil them.

She did not believe in lavishing luxuries upon them, but she did believe in furnishing such things, as would promote the health of the body and the growth of the mind. Unlike most colored parents, she realized that the mind was the most important part about her children, and she did not hesitate to purchase

books, instructive games and toys; things
that would cause her children to think and
study and do much toward their own self-
development. In other words she did not
starve the mind at the expense of the body.
She knew that both must be fed.

Thus Mrs. Simmons had brought to the
threshold of womanhood, a lovable, beautiful,
sensible, accomplished girl. A girl full of
health and vigor and buoyancy of spirit. A
girl whose training had not been neglected
in any line. Cooking, sewing and piano playing were her accomplishments and she was
very proud of her. No young woman could
have a greater asset to character or a greater
aid to future life and happiness than she,
with qualifications like these.

This morning she had just finished her
portion of the housework and had gone out
on the veranda to do deep breathing and other
exercises that she had found beneficial to
health. Through these exercises she had
learned the real secret of how to be healthful
and beautiful.

She remained there some time basking in
the June sunshine, gazing at nature everywhere arrayed in her most beautiful and at-
tractive garments.

"What is so rare as a day in June?
Then, if ever, comes perfect days;
Whether we look or whether we listen
We hear life murmurs or see it glisten."

She repeated to herself the above quotation, which was quite befitting. "Isn't that true?" she said, as she stooped and patted the large St. Bernard dog on the head, that lay happily at her feet. Ted never moved from his position, with his head resting between his paws, but rolled his eyes affectionately and wagged his bushy tail responsively, as if he understood her words and appreciated her happy, poetic frame of mind.

"You big noble boy," she murmured, and with a cheerful laugh she displayed an even set of ivory-like teeth, of which any queen might be proud. Then with a hop, skip and jump she hastened into the house to the side of her mother.

"Mother this is a grand day. I feel like strolling! If I were a poet I would write something. I am going to dress and go to the Public Library and get a good book, may I?" Her mother readily assented and it was not long before she was hastening along the shady side of the street toward the new Carnegie Library.

So pleased was she with the fresh morning air, perfumed as it were with blossoms

from nature's hot house, and with song and
twitter of birds and the steady rhythmic flow
of the majestic river, that she decided to pro-
long her walk, and take the path that led
along the river front.

She had not gone far, however, when she
saw a crowd of men and boys at a distance
and heard yells and clapping of hands. She
continued on her way until she had almost
reached the place of excitement. "Hit him
in the neck! Kill him! Now you got him!"
and other expressions told her that there
must be a fight in progress. At this moment
a small boy came running to her exclaiming,
"Miss Lillian! Your brother George is fighting. Him and Charley Christopher are having it! You had better come and stop it.
He's hurting George. George is just a
bleedin!"

When Lillian came upon the scene, the
boys were fighting like demons. Each, during his school career, had trained in athletic
sports, and was well prepared in self-defense.
Both knew the rough tactics resorted to in
Foot Ball games and they employed them in
this awful fight.

Both knew how to punch in a pugilistic
way and they were doing so. Side stepping,
swinging and uppercutting was indulged in
to the great delight and satisfaction of the

crowd. It was really a pretty fight to those
who loved a contest and knew anything about
pugilism. And but for the timely arrival of
Lillian it would perhaps have been a fight to
the finish.

The crowd slunk back when she approached, most of them knowing that she
was George's sister, and dropped their heads
and began to walk away.

"Shame on you George," she said, rush-
ing in and pulling him by the shoulders.
"What on earth is the matter with you?"

"Let loose sister, I am going to kill this
Southern nigger," said George, who was
breathing heavily and bleeding profusely at
the nose and mouth.

"You are going right home with me. I
am ashamed of you. What will papa and
mama say when they know of this?"

George was too tired or nervous to reply.
Charles Christopher, embarrased and cha-
grined at sight of George Simmons' beautiful
sister, turned with hung-down head to his
hat and coat, picked them up and walked
away.

George made one more effort as if to get
to him, then giving over to the remonstrances
of his sister reached for his coat and hat and
putting them on, remarked, "This is not done

with yet, you Southern dog. I'll get you some other day."

The fight had had its effect on him. He was considerably bruised and beaten. Both eyes were black and his face and ears were badly swollen. He was a sorry looking spectacle with his face and hands and clothing besmeared with blood, as he passed along the street.

After reaching home he attempted to explain to his mother and sister the cause of the fight. His mother, though sorry for him, was disgusted on account of his hot-headedness and his method of getting rid of Southern negroes. She too felt that they had been a menace to the community, and shared the opinion with the other Northern people that they were the cause of much of the prejudice that was now cropping out in their town. But being a very conservative woman and not given much to criticism or to the judging of others, had not given the matter very deep thought or consideration, had no suggestion whatever to offer.

George declared that he was going to continue along the lines that he had started until every objectionable character was gone. He said that he had many staunch friends that thought as he did, and he knew that they would help him.

"I don't know that I would take so much upon myself," said Lillian. "You may get the worst of it. Who is this fellow Christopher any way?" she asked. She wished to know more about a young man who could make her big strong brother, who starred on the Foot Ball team a season ago, look like that.

"Ah he is one of them smart Alex' from the South. He claims to be a College graduate. Think of a graduate from a Negro College."

"I was talking to some of the boys about Southern niggers coming up here and spoiling our privileges and he took it up. He brought up a lot of his Southern talk and argument and made me sore. So I told him to 'beat it' out of this town as soon as he could."

"Why you didn't tell him that, did you George?"

"I certainly did," said George.

"And what did he say?"

"Oh, he got dramatic and reared himself back and said, 'I had rather die a hundred deaths than to accede to your demand; you have insulted me, so now you've got to whip me,' or words to that effect. So we started from there. And if you had not come up and interfered I would have given him a good thrashing. I had him going and all I wanted was to land one more punch to make him take the count. He is an awful tough guy, though, but I'll get him yet."

"Stay out of trouble George," said his mother. "Keep away from such people. Nothing can be gained by associating with them. You have a superior education and a superior intellect and you should use them for something better than an argument or a street brawl with ignorant people. I would just stay away from him if I were you."

"Well mother if I let him off now he will think I am afraid of him. He has already said that he would remain here as long as he pleased. Such fellows just sow prejudice. They have already caused us to be barred from privileges in the parks. They have been the cause of our segregation in the theatres. We can't eat in the down town restaurants any more; and the next thing you know, we will have 'Jim Crow' street cars and perhaps separate schools."

George did not really believe that 'Jim Crow' street cars would be instituted in the North. But desiring to make his arguments effective, and to increase the prejudice in the hearts of his mother and sister against Southern colored people, he magnified probabilities and possibilities.

Then, remembering the defiant look in Charles Christopher's eyes, and recalling the questions that had underminded his own heretofore formidable arguments, together with the ability, which he had shown that morning to defend himself, and to resent insult, deep down in his heart, George felt that for the time he had been beaten. He was no quitter, however, and he was anxious for another opportunity. He was by no means convinced that Charles Christopher was his master, intellectually, physically or in any other way. He knew, though, that the Southern element in his city was quiet and conservative, only because they lacked leadership. That they had gained enough strength in late years to advocate and put through many of their Southern ideas, in contrast to the Northern ideas, regarding the solution of the race problem. And he felt that if Charles Christopher should assume the leadership of that element, that through his advocacy many constitutional rights of his people would be denied. So he concluded that he would nip the thing in the bud. That Charles Christopher must go.

Lillian said no more as it was her day to prepare dinner. And she knew that her father would be in soon.

Mrs. Simmons looked at her son sympathetically and said, "You had better go, now, and lie down awhile on the couch and rest yourself. We will tell father about it when he comes."

Mrs. Simmons, good woman that she was, shared in the belief of her son, and in her heart sprang a great dislike for Charles Christopher, though she knew nothing of him. She hated the idea of separate schools, and had often been heard to say that she would rather have her children grow up in gross ignorance than to have them taught in separate schools by colored teachers. She looked upon a negro college as a joke, and its graduates as ignoramuses. And if Charles Christopher was a representative of such a school, she knew that he could not amount to very much, and she did not want her son to associate with him or even stoop so low as to quarrel or fight with him. She was willing though, that he join hands with others and help rid the community of this Southern element, if such a thing were possible.

When Mr. Simmons came she took the responsibility of relating to him what had happened in the forenoon.

He was much wrought up, and declared that George had acted just right; that he would stand by him in whatever he undertook. He declared, that he had many friends, and some influence in that community, and that he would see whether this young upstart from the South could remain in that town as long as he wanted to or not.

He would notify his friends, call an indignation meeting, and see if the scamp could not be started a little sooner than he desired.

He would show him who was running that town.

Mr. Simmons, as already has been stated, was clerk in the City Treasurer's office. He was highly respected and did have considerable influence. He was looked upon as the leader of his people in the city and usually represented them on the civic questions that pertained to their interest. And in this case it would be an easy matter to get them together, as all thought much the same as he. And those who had different views were silent, fearing to express them, lest they might offend some of their neighbors, who in case they should would make life in the community a burden for them in the future. And as young George Simmons had surmised, it would take some one who had no special interest in the community, or love, or respect for its people, to lead an opposition.

So Mr. Simmons felt safe in calling an indignation meeting for the purpose of denouncing the objectionable Southerner.

When he was through eating his dinner, he went in the room where George was resting, and asked for his version of the fight. George told him all about it. After he was through, his father said, "I don't blame you, I am going to call the boys together soon and see what can be done about it."

"I thank you very much, father," said George, "I was quite sure you would approve of my action."

His father then departed, saying, "I will see you later about this matter."

Lillian, whose spirits were so high earlier that morning, and who saw so much beauty in nature and life, whose poetic soul revelled as it were, in what bade fair to be a perfect day, was now sad and cast down. Her heart was troubled. And she thought, "O, how transitory and fleeting is happiness."

After her duties of the noon hour were finished, she went into the room where her brother lay, and tried to say something that would comfort him. She knew that if he were not suffering physical pain, his pride was wounded. And had she been convinced that he would have conquered the young Southerner, she would almost wish that she had not interfered. She tried to feel that she hated Charles Christopher for what he had done to her brother.

The rest of the day was spent in meditating along this line and drawing mental pictures of the fight. Even to the setting sun, and after George had recovered himself enough to go out for a stroll, she was still thinking. And thus ended a well begun and beautiful June day for her.

CHAPTER III

THE NEWSPAPER ARTICLE.

Charles Christopher, save for a few scratches and a black eye, was none the worse for the fight. There was to him one embarrassing and unpleasant feature, however. The one that he regretted most; and that was the appearance of George's beautiful sister. If he could only meet her, and apologize, and explain things to her, he would be satisfied. But he knew that this would be impossible. She could never know his side of the story. She could never understand the cause for which he fought. There was no way for her to learn his true worth. His heart was big, and broad, and as true as steel. But she would go on through life mistrusting him, despising him, for what she considered a great wrong to her brother, and an insult to the community. All that was possible for him to do was to long to meet her and explain. But he could not hope to do so.

He now quickened his steps, for it was almost time to serve dinner at the hotel, where he was employed as a waiter. Putting on his apron he took his station at his table, and the first person to be seated was a reporter for the "Daily News." He knew Charles well and often joked with him. "Hello, boy!" he said. "Who poked you in the eye?" Charles told him about the fight, how it started and all. The story seemed to interest the reporter. He asked a few leading questions, wrote the answers on his note pad, and placed it in his pocket.

When he was through eating, he arose, slipped Charles a half-dollar, as was his custom, and said, "Watch the papers tomorrow, boy."

Charles thanked him and told him that he would. Charles did not think he could make so much out of what he considered a very small affair.

But the next morning the article appeared in the "Daily News," in glaring headlines as follows:

WAR BETWEEN THE NORTH AND SOUTH.

TWO YOUNG NEGROES REPRESENTING DIFFERENT SECTIONS FIGHT. SOUTHERN NEGROES CLAIM VICTORY.

The above headlines and the column and half article, that followed, stirred up the col-

ored citizens from center to circumference.
It literally set them wild.

As a rule, when colored people see anything in the paper, they take it very seri-
ously, and if it is about their own race, they
continue to discuss it for months afterward.

In this article the principals of the com-
bat were mentioned, and the cause which led
up to it, were given in detail. Continuing, it
said that the police were nowhere to be
found, and criticised them severely for allowing more than a hundred men and boys to
assemble and witness such a contest. "The
fight was stopped by the sister of the gentleman who stood up for the North. A riot
might have ensued had it not been for her
timely arrival. A riot once started it is hard
to tell where it might have ended. For some
time, the Northern Negroes, and the Southern
Negroes of the city, have been at dagger
points, over the subject of separate schools,
and the segregation question, falling some-
time into heated debates.

"The Northern Negroes also claim that
their rights and privileges in public places
have been denied them on account of the influx of the bad Negroes from the South, and
that they are going to take steps to try to
stop them from coming in the city. If such
steps are taken, more trouble is looked for."

When Charles picked up the paper and saw such an elaborate account of the affair, he was astounded.

"Who would have thought it?" said he. "Well I am in for it now; I guess the whole town will be on me." He did not figure on any sympathizers, outside of a few of the boys who were working at the Hotel.

He met the reporter just coming in for his breakfast. "For the love of Mike, man," he said. "You have put me in bad. These colored people here will lynch me."

"Why, what are they saying?"

"I haven't seen any of them yet, but I know about how they feel."

"Well, your people, Charles, are easily stirred up, but just as easy to quiet down. I don't think you need have any fear of them."

"I tell you, if anything happens or you hear of any trouble, you just let us know of it. We will take care of you."

With this he took his seat at the table and ordered his breakfast.

Charles served him, as usual, and when he had finished, and arose to go, he handed him the usual tip, patted him on the shoulder and said, "I did not mean to cause you trouble, Charles, but if I have, you may rest assured that I will stand by you. I am from the South myself. I know something about the true worth of the people down there. The noblest, the richest, the cream of the Negro race are down there."

Charles thanked him for his words of encouragement, but he could not help feeling a little uneasy. He thought that he knew the minds and hearts of the people much better than did the reporter.

The next morning, after a night of restlessness, of bad dreams and nightmares and fights, which she had attempted to stop in her sleep, Lillian Simmons arose and dressed. Her heart was still heavy. She had hoped to awake and find the happenings of the preceding day a horrible nightmare, like most persons have experienced, at some time in their lives. But her hopes were all in vain. The truth dawned only too clearly, and was verified when she picked up the morning paper and saw the glaring head-lines, that magnified and told of the unfortunate affair. Lillian almost swooned when she read the article, and came to the part that she played in the disgraceful affair. She ran into the house, clutching the paper to her breast with both hands, and with stifling cry, fell across her mother, who was yet in bed and slumbering feverishly.

She immediately awoke, exclaiming, "What on earth is the matter with my child?

What has happened?" She was awake, but it seemed an age before her senses would aid her in determining the trouble with her daughter. "Don't cry like that, Lillian. Something terrible must have happened to 'mother's baby.'"

Lillian was now choking and crying aloud, as if her heart would break. Mrs. Simmons, rising from bed, lifted her up, and such a pitiful expression she had on her face, she had never seen before. "Tell mother what's the matter, dear," she said, covering the face of Lillian with kisses. Lillian was so grieved that she could not speak. She simply pointed to the glaring headlines.

Mrs. Simmons read. As she continued, it was plain that she was affected. Being of a light complexion, one could easily note the changes in her countenance, anger and chagrin, each had its turn, as she read the details as published in the paper. And when she came to the part that Lillian played, she then knew the cause of her daughter's grief.

She tried to console her and treat the matter lightly. But Lillian would not be consoled. She felt that she was a part of the vulgar crowd that had assembled at the fight, that she was the object of public censure, and that she was disgraced forever. And as these thoughts came teeming in on her troubled mind, she grew hysterical, and her mother could do nothing with her.

Her ravings and loud cries brought the other members of the household, that is her father and brother, into the room and to her side.

Mrs. Simmons thrust the paper to them and told them to read. They did so, both the father and the son looking on at the same time.

When they had finished the article, the father tried to appear calm, but it was plain that a tempest raged within. He remarked, however, that he saw nothing in the article to cause Lillian to be carrying on as she was. To be able to break up a fight and cause a crowd to scatter like that, really stamped her as a heroine.

"Oh, do you really and truly think so, papa?" she said between sobs.

"Indeed I do, my girl. I am really proud of your action," he said, as he stooped and planted a kiss on her feverish brow.

"Well, papa, if you mean it I am happy. I shall not cry any more," she said, trying to brighten up. But in spite of the effort, the big tear drops continued to fall, and the childish whimperings she was unable to control.

George stood with hung down head and said nothing. But he was thinking a lot. And what he was thinking would not look well in a Sunday school book, nor on any printed page as to that matter.

To him the details of the fight, as published in the paper, contained not the semblance of truth. And he was quite sure that the information was furnished by Charles Christopher himself, or some of his Southern sympathizers. At some time he would make them swallow it in big doses. And with clinched fists, he gritted his teeth unobserved by the others and left the room.

"Something ought to be done about this," said Mrs. Simmons.

"Never fear, mother," said Mr. Simmons in reply. "Something will be done. And that very soon.

"I am going to call the citizens together this very night, and before twenty-four hours something will be done. Why, it's an outrage on the community." With this he left the room. And Lillian and her mother set about silently to prepare the morning meal. Both were very nervous and were trying to gain self-control.

At the breakfast table the article in the paper was not alluded to, so it was not very long before they each showed signs of cheerfulness, and were enjoying their breakfast of coffee, biscuits with butter, fried ham and potatoes. Mrs. Simmons could make the best of biscuits; she was an excellent cook.

CHAPTER IV

THE INDIGNATION MEETING.

After eating breakfast all felt better. The sting of the newspaper article gradually began to grow less painful. All four were sensible, well read pepole, and had long since learned that everything published in the papers was not true, that intelligent people did not so regard it. The consoling words that her father had spoken to her, acted like magic in the healing of Lillian's broken heart. And the rest of the day she felt comparatively well. She almost felt proud of the part she took in stopping the fight, because her father had said that it was the part of a heroine. So her grief had almost passed away.

The father and son left the house together. They went straight to one of the down town printing offices and had some hand bills struck, announcing a mass meeting for the colored citizens to be held at the Methodist church. Business of importance to be transacted. The meeting was called for eight o'clock that night. Nothing else was necessary to bring the people together. They had all heard about the fight and most of them had read the article in the paper. And all the Northern people thought alike, that something must be done. So at eight o'clock every seat in the church was taken. As was customary at such meetings, Capt. Simmons was made permanent chairman and Frank Wilson secretary.

Without further preliminaries Captain Simmons, who gained his title from some other source than a soldier's record, in an address announced the purpose of the meeting.

"Ladies and Gentlemen," said he amid breathless silence, "We have assembled here this night for a cause, the gravity of which can scarcely be comprehended. Much depends upon what we say here and what we do here tonight. Dark clouds are lowering and hanging heavily over us. And a storm that threatens to sweep us off the face of the earth is brewing. The question is, can we avert it? Can we escape it?

"You all know what has transpired in the past two days, and the cause which brought about the unpleasant affair as well as I. You have seen the morning paper. And each one of you have had your say regarding it. We have expressed ourselves privately on the question ofttimes before and have had

some pretty clear cut ideas as to what ought
to be done. But we are here tonight to express in a public way our views and ideas; to
organize and form some definite plan of procedure. We do not wish in any way to dis-
guise the fact that we are indignant at the
insult and humiliations that are being heaped
upon us each day in increasing measures. We
are indignant at our daily paper for publishing such an article, and coloring it in the
manner in which it did, this morning. Cast-
ing a reflection on our manhood and integrity,
and attempting to discourage us in our
struggle for higher ideals and good citizen-
ship. Yes, we are indignant. We are indignant at a certain undesirable element from
another section of this country who have
come among us and who have brought with
them habits and ideas that are a menace to
this community, and a detriment to the welfare of the colored citizenry, and we have
assembled here this night for the purpose of
taking positive steps toward ridding ourselves of this undesirable element, and to try
to secure redress for some of the wrongs already inflicted upon us. This is an indignation meeting; all are allowed to express themselves, and it is requested by the Chair that
as many as can will do so. I have placed the
matter before you, act wisely and deliber-

ately. I think I need not say more. What is
the further pleasure of the house?" he asked,
as his gavel fell heavily upon the table before
him.

"Mr. Chairman," a dozen voices spoke,
as a dozen men arose to their feet simul-
taneously.

"The Chair is in doubt," said the speaker.
"All please be seated."

"Mr. Chairman." A dozen men sprang
up as before. The Chair, realizing the diffi-
culty of trying to give the first man on his
feet an opportunity to speak, tried the next
best plan of procedure, that is of recognizing
the one furthest off.

"Mr. Washington has the floor," he said,
as he lifted his eyes beyond those nearest him.

Capt. Simmons was a skillful parliamen-
tarian, and possessed much executive ability,
and was well fitted for the position which he
now held.

"To what did you arise, Mr. Washington?"

"Mr. Chairman, I arise to make a motion.
There is really nothing before the house, and
in order to get things started, I move that
we proceed to the regular order of business
for which we have assembled."

"I second the motion, Mr. Chairman,"
said the nearest man to Washington.

"It has been moved and seconded that we proceed to the regular order of the business in hand. Are you ready for the question?"

"Question!" A number of voices rang out through the house.

"Those who are in favor of said motion let it be known by the usual sign, aye."

"Aye!" The whole house shouted. "Contrary, Nay."

"The motion carries by an unanimous vote," said the chairman, "and we will now proceed to the discussion of the business before the house."

"Mr. Chairman," said Frank Maxwell, who was very anxious to talk, and who showed great signs of excitement, "I arise to a question of privilege."

"Mr. Maxwell has the floor," said the chairman. "Proceed Mr. Maxwell."

"Mr. Chairman, Ladies and Gentlemen of this assembly, I have lived in this city for twenty-five years. I have seen the town grow from a small village of two thousand people to its present size. I know when the spot whereon this building now stands, was a vine-clad forest, a fit hiding place for the wild. I have watched people come and I have watched them go, but through all the vicissitudes and changes that time has wrought, I have never known such bold effrontery to manhood, such wanton and reckless trampling of ideals and principles underfoot, as is being practiced in our midst today.

"Are we to sit idly and see our rights and privileges one by one slip from us, when it is in our power to prevent? Are we going to waste the time away in useless words, spoken where they have no weight, where they are as seed sown on stony ground, or are we, like men, going to take decided steps tonight against further injury or further insult? Who in this assembly is willing to shed precious blood, yes, lay down his life for this cause that is vital, one might say, to our very existence? I for one am ready to fight to get things right. And I hope that every true, loyal citizen of the North is willing to take a stand and prepare for the task of ridding the community of this undesirable rabble that has come into our midst, and has been the cause of our recent and previous troubles; and the denying to us of our constitutional rights."

Maxwell, as may have been observed by the reader through his speech, was an educated man. He had also completed a course in law in a Northern college and had at one time belonged to the Bar Association. But on account of a lack of practice, he was forced to abandon the profession, and at fifty without the care of a family, he was custodian of one of the large down town bank buildings. He, however, was highly respected by both races, and was active in church work, secret organizations, politics and civic affairs in general. He was an eloquent, fiery speaker, and was able to play upon the emotions of his hearers, thus arousing them and eliciting hearty and frequent applause.

He spoke at length and being a lawyer used many technical terms, language of his own profession, dwelling much on constitutional rights, and the fourteenth and fifteenth articles of amendments. Then soaring away on the wings of eloquence, to heights of oratory, seldom attained by ordinary men, he concluded his speech with the thrilling words of Patrick Henry, "Give me liberty or give me death," and took his seat amid a storm of applause that shook the very foundation upon which the building stood.

Many others expressed themselves much along the same lines, but none surpassed him in eloquence and beauty and clearness of thought.

The chairman, after many good and otherwise speeches were made in keeping with the spirit of the meeting, suggested that the hour was growing late, and that the discussion might well be closed at that time for the purpose of formulating some definite

plans of procedure. That he was ready to
entertain suggestions or motions along that
line. "But first," said he, "By virtue of my
office as chairman of this meeting, I shall proceed to appoint two committees, one to draw
up resolutions in keeping with the spirit and
purpose of this meeting, the other as a committee on vigilance, whose duty will be
definitely expressed later on."

The first committee that he appointed
consisted of five men, with Frank Maxwell as
chairman, which immediately left the room
to begin its work.

The vigilance committee was made up of
ten able-bodied men who retired to another
room and organized with George Simmons as
its leader or Chairman.

The Chairman announced that while the
committees were out at work he would entertain any one who might yet desire to express
himself. "Would be glad to have a word from
some of the ladies," he said.

The ladies were all backward when it
came to talking in public, and none of them
seemed to show a desire to speak.

Mrs. Simmons and Lillian were there,
and sat together listening attentively to every
word that was said. They were carried away
with the speech-making, and it seemed that
Captain Simmons' words spoken that morn-

ing before breakfast were about to come true.

Mrs. Simmons told some of the ladies of Lillian's troubles that morning. They pitied her so much, for Lillian was beloved by all. But they assured her, as her father had done, that there was no harm done whatever. So they laughed and chatted gaily until the committee on resolutions returned and announced that it was ready to report.

The resolutions were read and seemed to meet the approval of the assembly. They seemed to be the only remedy that would cope with the conditions as they now stood. First of all they condemned the morning paper for publishing such an article as it had that morning, and recommended that it be asked to refute the statement, or that they be allowed to give their version of what had happened the day before. They denounced the Southern Negro as being an undesirable citizen, that his ideas and cowardly ways tended to create prejudice. That the rougher element from the South had caused, through his bad conduct, many of their rights and privileges to be denied them.

They further recommended that the vigilant committee appointed by the chairman see to it that no more undesirables be permitted to come into the community. And those who were there were to be held in restraint.

That the young ruffian, Charles Christopher, who made the vicious attack on one of their most worthy and scholarly young men, be asked to leave the city at once. If not through persuasion, then by force. These were the most important things embodied in the resolutions.

"You have heard the resolutions, what is your pleasure?"

"Mr. Chairman," the voice came from the women's side of the house. "Mrs. Lester," said the chairman.

"Mr. Chairman, I move that the resolutions be received and adopted."

Mrs. Lester was loudly applauded for her action, and was seconded by a dozen men.

"You have heard the motion to receive and adopt the resolutions, are you ready to vote," cried the chairman.

"Not ready!"

All turned in the direction of the old gray-headed speaker at the door.

"Brother Littlejohn, state your reasons for not being ready," said the chairman.

"Wall, Mr. Chairman, I am not ready kase I thinks youall wrong. In de fust place dem air resolutions condemnin' Southern folks is wrong. You all up here in de Norf seem to think that the cullud folks ob de Souf has caused all de troubles. But youse wrong.

Hit is de natchul feelin' dat one class or race of people has agin annudder, lack you all showed here tonight! Hits as natchul for white folks to not like cullud folks and make laws agin' 'em, and impose upon 'em, as it is for you all to not lack Southern cullud folks and 'pose 'pon dem."

"Brother Littlejohn, you must be brief," said the chairman as he moved uneasily in his chair. "The hour is growing late. Confine your speech to the resolutions."

"Now, Mr. Chairman, don't commence anything like dat. Be fair, you all has had your say, now give poor old pappie a chance.

"I know that ise an ignorant old man, can't say things proper lack de rest ob you. Kase I has no book larnin', I hasn't been to school, I hasn't had de chance dat you has had. But I has some mother's wit, and some common sense and I knows when a thing is right or wrong. So please give me a chance to 'spress myself.

"I was borned in de Souf and I can't set still here and say nothin' in 'fense of it. Dey is just as 'spectable down dar as you all is up here, and dey has more money, more property and more pride than you all has. And when you pass resolutions 'hibitin' colored folks of de Souf from comin' here youse doin' wrong. I has lived in dis here town for seventeen

"When you cast 'flections on de Souf, you cast
'flections on me."

years, and me and my family has been as
'spectable as any of you. And when you cast
'flections on de Souf you cast 'flections on me.

"If you all wants a voice and wants to
measure arms wid de white man, you has to
get somethin' of your own.

"Colored folks own dis buildin', don't
dey? Will any white man dare to come in
here and kick you aroun' an' impose 'pon
you? No! Why? Kase he reco'nizes owner-
ship. You can tell a white man whar to set
in dis church, kase its yourn. The white man
tells you whar to set in de theatres an' in de
railroad trains kase dey is hisn. He bars you
from privileges in de Parks and Hotels kase
he owns dem and can do what he pleases wid
'em. Den you colored folks here in de Norf
try to put the blame on the Southern Negro,
when it is jest a case of might makin' right.
The stronges' race takin' a stand agin the
weaks, the white blood assertin' itself and
puttin' forth efforts to hold in check other
races and have de bes' things for itself.

"An if you Negroes ever 'mount to anything you got to git togedder like de Negroes
of de Souf has been forced to do. Have some
stores an' banks an' parks an' theatres an'
some schools ob your own. Don't wait till de
white folks kick you out an den blame de bad
Negroes from de Souf for it.

"An' annudder thing you is wrong in, you has de same spirit in you dat de mob has in de Souf. If you drives dis man out of town you can't criticise de white men who lynch Negroes in de Souf. You is full of prejudice yourself and you can't expect people to deal fair wid you unless you hab it in your own hearts to be fair wid others.

"An' now Mr. Chairman, I am through and I thank you an' de ladies an' de gentlemen, for given me 'der respectful 'tention. You can do what you please. I has been settin' here listening to de speeches, an' watchin' de proceedin's, an' when I know dat you is doin' wrong, I wouldn't be much of a man to set still an' say nothin'. I feel now that I has done my Christian duty. How can de Negro race ever 'mount to much when dey is fightin' agin one nother? What more can you expect of de other race when we has so much prejudice in our own hearts? The color line is drawn in our own race. Yaller Negroes think dey is better den black ones. Northern Negroes think dey is better den Southern Negroes. Lord help us to get right."

"Your time is up," said the Chairman, striking his gavel on the table.

Old man Littlejohn took his seat. It was some time before any one spoke. It seemed that they had swallowed and were now trying to digest old man Littlejohn's speech.

"Are you ready to vote on the resolutions?" said the Chairman finally.

"Just a word, Mr. Chairman," said Maxwell, who had risen to the floor. He did not want the audience to feel that the old gentleman's speech was worthy of an answer, yet he was afraid to ignore it, lest it had gone straight to the hearts of a majority who had their origin in the South, and whose sympathies were with the South, but who heretofore had kept silent about it, either ashamed or afraid to confess it. For there was some logic and some truth in what the old man said.

So he began: "Mr. Chairman, it is just such cowardly talk that makes the Southern Negro objectionable. He is positively detrimental to his own good, and to ours also. There never was a nation that ever amounted to anything, who did not take matters into their own hands, and strike the first blow for their rights. We are after our rights, Mr. Chairman, our constitutional rights, and we cannot afford to allow such people as these to deter us in our efforts.

"I am quite sure though that every one sees the matter in the proper light, and will vote for the resolutions. We cannot and will not be blinded by ignorance and superstition."

At this juncture the chairman put the motion which carried by a safe majority. He then instructed the Vigilance Committee as to its duty, requesting that it carry out the things recommended in the resolutions to the letter.

After which the meeting adjourned until conditions should require another.

CHAPTER V

THE WARNING HEEDED

That night George Simmons trudged homeward chuckling in glee at the advantage he now held over Charles Christopher. "And I am going to use it, too," thought he. "I'll show him that he can't come up here talking his Southern talk and get by with it."

So he went to his room and lay until morning, planning a sweet revenge against Charles Christopher. The rest of the family were soon wrapt in slumber, not being used to such unusual hours for retiring.

But Lillian, like her brother, lay awake the greater portion of the time. In spite of all her efforts she could not dismiss the words of old man Littlejohn's speech from her mind. In fact his was the only one she could remember distinctly. 'Tis true she was carried away by the eloquence and flowery talk of Frank Maxwell, but really when she came to think about it, he had left no deep thoughts over which her mind might ponder. But old man Littlejohn's advice for united effort, his advice to cleanse the heart of prejudice, or

65

secret faults, of injustice did mean something.

Was it not true that her brother, at the head of the vigilant committee, was the same as the man who leads a band of lynchers in the South, who burns the homes of innocent and helpless Negroes? Was it not the purpose of this committee to condemn without trial certain misguided persons of their own race? Was it not their intention to drive Charles Christopher from the city if he insisted on his right to remain? Was it in obedience to the Golden Rule, "Do unto others as you would have them do to you?" Was it a Christian-like spirit?

Surely old man Littlejohn's talk had its effect, to cause all these questions to come teeming into Lillian's youthful mind for fair, unbiased answers. Child as she was, she had the sense of justice planted deeply in her nature. She had individuality, she had character, and best of all, moral courage. And like old man Littlejohn, she could not sit still and see the wrong asserting itself without protesting against it.

Was there any way that she could prevent the wrongs which were about to be perpetrated in this case? Could she in any way prevent her brother from doing something that for the time might satisfy and heal his wounded pride, but in years to come might burn into his conscience and cause eternal suffering? Old man Littlejohn so far wrong in the use of the vehicles of speech, untrained in book lore, unschooled in the theories of law as given to the world by Blackstone, ignorant of social codes or parlor etiquette, was not wrong at heart. He had the true principles of moral philosophy deeply planted in his nature. And Lillian so regarding it determined to stand on the platform that he had laid down. It was not fair to hold a race accountable for wrong acts committed by certain individuals of that race. And the fact that the white people of their town were doing this, stamped them as unfair and unjust, and old man Littlejohn was right when he advanced the theory that it was the natural spread of prejudice which would have come sooner or later regardless of the influx of the Southern Negro.

Lillian lay till morning pondering over these thoughts. She loved her brother dearly and sympathized with him, but she felt that he was in the wrong. She felt that they were all in the wrong. And she was going to try to prevent them from putting their wrong ideas into practice. She did not want her brother to do things that he would regret in later life.

So she decided to see Charles Christopher
and persuade him to leave the city before the
committee should command him to do so.
And if he should do so, he perhaps would
save himself untold trouble, and her brother
George would not be charged with having
done a member of his race an injustice. So
deciding she arose at the usual hour and went
about her morning duties.

That morning at the breakfast table they
all showed some signs of fatigue, and of being
affected by the late hours kept the night before, with perhaps the exception of George.
He looked rather bright and fresh.

"How did you all like the meeting last
night," he said. "Wasn't it grand?"

"I was well pleased," said Mrs. Simmons.

Captain Simmons brightened up at the
mention of the meeting. He took great pride
in being a leader in the community, and considered himself highly honored, when called
upon to preside, which was done nearly at
all times.

"Well," he said, "I told you yesterday
morning, that before twenty-four hours,
something would be done. Didn't I tell you
all that, mother? The conduct of the people
was excellent," he continued. "I never pre-

sided over a body that was as easily controlled as that was last night."

"Well, the fact is the boys have got their
minds made up to stop all this heathenism,
and when you get the people all to be of one
mind, they come together for business, they
don't have time for so much foolishness, and
they are easily handled. The only thing that
had a tendency to mar the meeting was old
man Littlejohn up there with his ignorance,"
said George. "If I had been in your place,
father, I would have sat him down."

"I think your father did the right thing
to let him talk. He is a good old man and
no one paid any attention to his ignorance.
It's well to humor such people," said Mrs.
Simmons.

"Yes, mother, but we didn't have time to
listen to his foolishness. He would be amus-
ing on the stage, but we were not rendering
a vaudeville program there last night."

"George, you ought to be ashamed to
make sport of the old man that way. I
listened closely to him and I think he was
right in most all he said. One thing about it,
I can remember more of what he said, than I
can of Maxwell. I think he is right when he
says that colored people should not fight
against each other," said Lillian, aiming to
work up to the place where she could question

George as to what he intended to do in the case of Charles Christopher. But she found out through George's next remark.

"Well, I know this much, we are going to fix that Charles Christopher. I think he will be 'bully' enough to refuse to go when we ask him. I hope he will, because then we will have the fun of making him go. We are going to give him just three days in which to get ready and if he doesn't go in that length of time he will wish he had."

"When are you going to inform him that he must leave?" asked Lillian.

"We are going to inform him this very afternoon at four o'clock. He will be off from work at that time. He is off this morning at ten, but we can't get the boys together at that hour."

"Is the whole committee of ten going to wait on him?" asked Captain Simmons.

"No, there will be only three of us go to him. But if he refuses the whole ten will take part."

Lillian said no more, but she was figuring what excuse she would make to get away from the house. For she was now more determined than ever to thwart the plans of the committee which she considered no better than a mob. Ten able-bodied men against one man seemed cowardly to her. As soon as breakfast was over she would find some kind of excuse to get away and warn Charles Christopher. Not to save him, but to save her brother from a dastard act which meant a seared conscience to him in after life.

She would go to the library and get the book that she failed to get on the day of the fight.

"Mother, may I go to the library this morning and get my book? I am lonely and want something to read." She thus addressed her mother, after her morning duties were performed.

"Yes, dear, but don't stay long," was the reply from her mother.

So she dressed as prettily as she could and started.

The morning after the indignation meeting, when Charles Christopher came out of the Hotel, he went, as he was accustomed to do, to the river bank. It was here where he had chanced to hear the words that had stirred up so much strife.

He took his usual seat and began to watch life as enacted on and near the river. It was a beautiful morning, almost as beautiful as the preceding day, with its stage set with natural splendor, the earth bedecked with flowers, the distant forest dressed in its newest garb, made lively by the songs of birds flitting gleefully about. And Charles Christopher, inspired by the surroundings, began to muse sweetly to himself. He had almost forgotten the unpleasant event of the preceding day. But he had not forgotten the beautiful angelic face of Lillian. "A creature of the day," he thought. "A fairy fit only for beautiful days and lovely scenes like this. Why is she forced to mingle with ordinary mortals like us? But since she must, then it is my right to love and admire her and long and hope, if I dare, for acquaintance and friendship with her. I would give almost anything could I see her and speak to her now and pour out my heart yearnings at her feet, turn my soul inside out, as it were, that she might see its purity, that she might understand and behold its true mechanism. To know and understand my heart would be to forgive the wrong that she must imagine that I have inflicted upon her brother. But some day, somewhere, somehow, I can not guess now, but things will be adjusted. The eternal truth must triumph, and Lillian Simmons will know the truth and moreover, accept the love I have for her."

As he mused thus, he heard a light tread in the soft grass near him. He looked up and behold the idol of his dreams was at his side.

Charles was dumbfounded. He could not believe his own eyes. His heart for the moment ceased to beat. Heavy drops of perspiration stood on his upturned brow, and his dark brown velvet skin had on it the paleness of death. A messenger from the tomb could not have surprised him more. Lillian, with her library book in hand, also showed some embarrassment, but the purpose for which she came gave her self-control, so she greeted him, saying, "This is Mr. Christopher, is it not?"

"It is," replied Charles with quivering lips.

"Well, Mr. Christopher, I come to see you on some very grave and important business. You no doubt have heard of the big indignation meeting held by the citizens of this town last night."

"I have not," stammered Charles truthfully.

"Well, there was one," continued Lillian "and one of its orders was that a vigilant committee, of which my brother is chairman, see that you leave this town. The committee consists of ten determined men, with whom you stand no possible chance singlehanded. And you will have serious trouble if you resist them or refuse to go when they command you. I know that you are no coward, Mr.

Christopher, but the best thing for you to do is to take my advice and leave town at once."

Charles looked up into the beautiful face of the young girl and said, "Miss Simmons, for I think that must be your name, I have done nothing to merit such treatment as this of which you speak. 'Tis true that your brother and I had an altercation day before yesterday, but he was as much in fault as I." And Charles related to her in his own way, the details which led up to the fight. "And I was very much embarrassed, Miss Simmons," he continued, "when you appeared upon the scene and separated us. I wanted to apologize to you," he said, as he stared at her with his large brown eyes, "but I had no chance, and feared that the chance would never come."

"Why, you owe me no apology, Mr. Christopher, you have done nothing to me and as for my brother, I am sure that he can do no more to you than you can do to him," said Lillian, reddening. "But my brother with nine other men can do you much harm. My brother is young and impetuous and is likely to do something that he might regret to the longest day he lives. And to save himself from a dastardly, cowardly, unmanly, though thoughtless act, is why I come to you as I do. And as I must not be seen talking to you, and

you can readily understand why, you are
sensible," she said betraying a degree of confidence in her tone of voice. "I must ask you
for a hasty reply. Will you leave for my
sake?"

Charles could no more resist the pleadings of Lillian Simmons than he could dam
up the great Niagara. So looking at her with
soft eyes that seemed to melt her very soul,
with eyes that spoke volumes unexpressed by
the lips, he said, "If I go as you ask, may I
hope—"

He did not finish, but she seemed to
understand him, and answered in tender accents. "Go do what I ask you for my sake,
and be a good boy. We do not know what the
future holds for us. I must go now, good-
bye." And before Charles could get himself
together and say the things that he most desired to say, the opportunity that he could
scarcely have hoped for, had come and gone.
He sat and watched her as she swiftly and
gracefully moved away. He watched her
even until she disappeared around the bend
in the flower strewn path and was hidden by
a thick cluster of shrubs and trees. For a
time he was bewildered. He was completely
overcome by Lillian's beauty and grace, and
by her earnest, yet tender plea. Her voice
was like sweet music to his ears and siren

like, she had lured him and won him to her
purpose.

Finally awakening to his senses he began
to think what he had done, what promise he
had made. Was it not cowardly for him to
leave at this particular time, when these
Northern people could and should be taught
a lesson? What would those of his sympathizing friends say and think of him? What
would the reporter, the manager of the hotel,
and many of the guests who had heard of the
affair say, should he leave at this time in
obedience to Lillian? But did she not give
him cause to hope? Was not the hope held
out in tender and confidentially spoken words
worth the sacrifice? "Go do what I ask you
for my sake and be a good boy." Did not
these words spoken by the beautiful Lillian
mean that there was at least a fighting chance
for him to win her love? Could he not go
away now and at some future time return and
say the things that he desired so much to say
to her? If he should leave the town for her
sake, to save the conscience of her brother in
the future, there would at least be common
grounds for friendship, and having an advantage like this, could he not follow it up
and seek to know her better? After thinking along this line for some time he finally
concluded that he would run the risk of being

called a coward for an opportunity like this.
He would go to the reporter and manager of
the Hotel, and as many of his friends as he
could find and explain the reasons for his de-
parture, as best he could, and would take the
first train out.   Then he remembered the
command of George Simmons, and his own
reply, "I had rather die a hundred deaths
than to heed or listen to your command."
"But this would not be obeying the command
of George Simmons," he thought; rather it
would be granting the request of his beautiful
sister whom he loved, and robbing George of
his opportunity for what he called a sweet
revenge.

The first train left the city at one thirty
that afternoon and Charles Christopher left
with it, disregarding the pleadings and im-
portunities of his friends.

CHAPTER VI

Thwarted

Lillian hastened toward home and as she trudged along she began to think of what she had done. This was the first time that she had done anything that she must conceal from her mother. The thought began to prey upon her mind. Being of a sensitive nature, and having been taught to never conceal anything from her mother, she found herself regretting her action. If she could only tell her about it, tell her why and all, she would feel satisfied, feel that her action was entirely right and proper. She felt, too, that her mother would approve of her action if she knew it. She knew that she loved George and had already cautioned him to stay out of trouble, and no doubt would have tried to prevent him herself, but perhaps she never would have thought of the plan that she had so successfully pursued. But would Charles Christopher have listened to her mother as he had listened to her? She believed not. She could not help knowing that Charles Christopher admired her. She had read that in his large,

78

soulful eyes, and that was why he had obeyed her. But would a plea from her mother have had the same effect on him? She believed not and felt somewhat flattered on the account of this fact. She had saved her brother from further trouble and kept a stain off his character by persuading Charles Christopher to leave, and she would not worry. Besides, Charles Christopher was a fine looking man, and his frank manner, his correct use of English, and his deep soulful eyes, which had expressed volumes to her, had impressed her. She liked him, that is why she spoke so tenderly to him, pleading with him to do her bidding, and encouraging him in the manner in which she did. She would always remember him and she would be kind to him, yes very kind to him if she should ever chance to meet him again. If he would write to her—

She was now ascending the steps of the veranda. The large St. Bernard met her and showed her his pleasure at her arrival by barking good naturedly and capering around her. She stopped, as was her custom, patted him on the head and said kind words to him, failing to complete her last thought in words, the large dog having interrupted.

"You back, Lillian?" asked her mother, as she entered the house. "I hope you were able to secure your book this time."

"Yes, mother, I have it. I am going to read it and tell you about it after dinner," said Lillian nervously.

"Hurry up and prepare the table dear, it is almost noon and your father will be here shortly."

Lillian said nothing, but bathing her face and hands, began her duties. And it was not long before the family was seated at the table. Captain Simmons was very complacent, but George seemed rather disturbed.

"George, what is the matter with you?" asked his mother at length.

"Oh, I am sore, mother. Don't you know," he continued, "I went to the Daily News office this morning and gave them our side, or our version of the fight the other day, and the editor threw it in the waste basket, said it was stale stuff, and they could not use it."

"So I up and told him the article they published was false, that it misrepresented the Northern colored people, and placed them in a bad light and we wanted it straightened out." 'We think it fair,' said I, 'that the public know our side of the affair, since it has gone so far. We did not have the least doubt that you would refuse us a hearing.' He said nothing, so I asked him if they would be willing to retract then, some of the things that were published. His reply was, 'Ah that is all past now, and we have no more time to fool with it. You colored people must try to get along together. You are always fighting among yourselves, that's why you lose out in so many things. There is strength only in unity. You ought to know that, George, you've been to school. My advice is for you to let it drop.' I was so angry I could not say another word. I just turned around and walked out."

Lillian listened and noted how disgusted and humiliated George seemed to be. She reddened perceptibly when he referred to Charles Christopher, the southern dog, as being the cause of it. "That's all such people are good for," he said. "Well, we will get him this afternoon. He will not get another chance to report lies to the paper and prejudice it against its own home people. This is the first time the paper has ever been unfair to us."

Mrs. Simmons, after hearing him through, said to him in her patient, tender, consoling accents. "Well son, you must not take things so hard. You must learn to be calm under fire. I think you are a little bit too radical. You are extreme in your likes and dislikes. You are either on the mountain top or in the valley. This morning you were

highly pleased, you fairly gloated over the
results of the meeting, and the advantages
that it gave you over your enemy. Now you
go to pieces because you have lost one point.
Your spirits seem to be groveling in the very
lowest depths of depression. You will have
to do better than that, my son. Don't allow
your hopes to rise too high or sink too low.
Try and strike a happy medium. You will be
happier if you adopt this plan."

George said no more, but it was plain to
be seen that he was very much displeased at
this turn of affairs.

Captain Simmons, not wishing to betray
his anger and his nervous excitement, after
Mrs. Simmons' pointed, but all too true remarks, remained silent throughout the meal.
When he was through eating, he arose from
the table abruptly, saying to George: "Be
sure and see that that young pup leaves this
town this afternoon," and started to his office.

"You may bet your last dollar on that,
father," said George revengefully. "I am
going after the boys now."

That afternoon at four o'clock George
and his committee stood at the hotel entrance
waiting for Charles Christopher to come out.
When told by some of the other employees
that Charles had left town he did not believe
them, and told them as much. He told them

that the pup need not be hiding, that he would have to come out some time. At this one of the boys remarked: "You don't think he is afraid of you do you? Why that boy can whip all three of you fellows. We would not lie to you George. He really is gone. He left on the one thirty train. He says that he is going further North."

"Boys don't be 'kidding,'" said George. "We are here for business. And we must see him. Tell him to come out, that we want to talk to him."

"Ask the proprietor if you don't believe us," said one of the boys. "I saw him when he got his time."

George was not satisfied with the report obtained from the boys, so he went to the hotel office and found the proprietor and told him that he wished to see Charles Christopher. The proprietor told him that Charles Christopher had gone. He then asked George, what was the matter with the colored people. "Why Charles Christopher is one of the best boys that I have ever had around here. And I hear that you people want to get rid of him. He is a whole lot better than you people who are fighting him. He is well educated, industrious, fine looking, good natured and everything else that goes toward the making of a perfect gentleman. I am surprised at your family opposing a fellow like him. I tell you right now that you are hurting yourselves in doing so."

"Pardon me, Mr. Dover," said George, attempting a defense, for he knew that such words coming from Clarence Dover, the proprietor of the Hotel, meant something, and if he could rid his mind of such ideas, he would be doing his people a great favor. Dover was one of the best friends the colored people had. He carried no prejudice in his heart for them, and would often accommodate them in his Hotel when they had the means to pay for it. His help was mixed. He considered one man as good as another. He recognized no creed, no color, no standard except that of manhood and good character. And to hear him talk like that had a tendency to dampen George's ardor and to cool his hot head.

"You do not understand the situation as we do."

"Situation or no situation," said Mr. Dover, "I know a good man when I meet one, and I don't believe in allowing them to be imposed upon. And if that boy had remained with me and you had harmed him, you and your people would have had to suffer for it. I have heard all about this affair. I tried to persuade him not to go. But he left because he did not want to cause you colored people trouble."

"Well, Mr. Dover," said George, "you are not in a mood to talk today, but I do hope at some time to be able to explain everything to you."

"I shall never be in a mood to listen to anything you have to say against Charles Christopher," replied Mr. Dover. "So you need never return on a mission like that."

"Well, good day Mr. Dover. I hope no harm has been done."

"Good day," replied the proprietor.

George left the hotel office feeling badly. He realized that he had over stepped his bounds by approaching the Hotel proprietor for such a purpose as he had. A sort of sheepish uneasy feeling came over him and a kind of choking sensation was in his throat. He felt for the first time that the young Southerner had bested him, but he would never confess it to anyone. He would make it appear that Charles Christopher, the cowardly Southern pup, fearing the thrashing that he had stored away in his sleeve for him, had left the city. He would make this boast so strong that other Southern Negroes would take warning and remain quiet. After all some good would come of his heading the vigilant committee, which was now a permanent organization. Consoling himself with this last thought he boastingly informed the other two young men who were with him of Charles' escapade, dismissed them and sneaked home by an unfrequented path, unobserved.

The discussion and feverish excitement continued for some time, but the serious trouble was averted by the timely withdrawal of Charles Christopher from the city. And sweet Lillian Simmons was the peace maker.

CHAPTER VII

THE TWO ARGUMENTS

There is, as is well known, a wide difference of opinion as to what is the best policy to pursue in solving what is called the race problem. The opinions are largely sectional, and so far as the colored race is concerned, are as wide apart as the two sections themselves. They are opposite. The colored people of the North being radical, believe in fighting with gun and sword, if need be, for their constitutional rights and privileges, while the colored people of the South believe in pursuing a more conservative course, securing rights and privileges through strategy or diplomacy or meritorious effort. How far either section is right, it is not our purpose to affirm or deny. We are forced to acknowledge though, that both policies as pursued by the different sections seem either to have failed or are very slow in attaining the desired results.

The Northern people abhor the idea of separate schools, yet they are being instituted year after year. City after city is

adopting the system. The fighting policy of
the Northern colored people seems to be in-
adequate to prevent or avert the almost constant spread or increase of the segregation
idea in its many forms. The Northern colored people argue that in the first place separate schools are unconstitutional, and are
not in keeping with the principles of liberty
and free government. They think the same
regarding the "Jim Crow" car, the segregation or setting of colored people in certain
districts of a city or town in which to dwell,
so that they may not come in too close contact with persons of the other race. They
argue that any tendency to deny or disre-
gard, or to set aside the law that acknowl-
edges the equality of man to man, is unfair
and unjust, that freedom is man's birthright,
that he should preserve his God given heri-
tage at any cost or at any hazard.

That he who would not is a coward void
of manhood and principle, and deserves all
the hardships and depression which he has
heaped upon him.

They claim that the race problem will
never be solved until the white race makes
up its mind to be fair with the colored race.
They claim that there would be no race problem if they had the sense of justice in their
hearts. They think that it will take force to

get them in the right attitude, and when the negroes, North and South, become a unit on this thought, no power or people on earth can impose upon them. That the idea, "He who would be free must fight," is divine. The North could not conquer the South until it promised freedom to the slaves. The slaves could not be free until they made up their minds to be slaves no longer and struck a blow in their own behalf. John Brown could do nothing for the Negro because their minds at that time were not pregnant with a determination to be free.

Abraham Lincoln, that far-seeing statesman, that diplomat, that instrument in God's hand, caught the idea in the air as it were, that "He who would be free must fight," and placed weapons of war in the hands of Negro men and boys, bidding them to free themselves.

You Southern people, says the North, argue that you have no guns, no ammunition, no power, by which you may obtain your rights. That is not it. You have no courage. You will not make the attempt because you are afraid that you will die. You are not willing to sacrifice life in the defense of that which is yours by inheritance. Come and join us, colored brothers of the South, not sectionally, but take on our spirit, imbibe our ideas for fair play and help us to teach the people of the other race there is no other solution of the race problem except fair treatment. Let us unite soul and body on the determination to get justice in this land at any cost and the battle is half won. God in his infinite wisdom, in his own mysterious way, will do the rest."

This is the doctrine that is preached by nearly all native colored people throughout the North. This is the idea that they would inculcate in the minds of the colored people from the South who come to dwell among them. This is the platform upon which the Simmons family stood. And this is what George Simmons wanted Charles Christopher to understand and to do.

But if Charles Christopher had had an opportunity to voice the sentiment of his people, he would have answered with the same stubborn facts, that all intelligent colored people from the South do when confronted with the boasting and fighting spirit of the North. "No doubt but what you are right, my brother, but does this agitation, this fighting policy which you recommend, ward off or even hold in check this unfair and unjust treatment, of which you so passionately and indignantly prate? We have segregation in all its odious forms forced upon us. We are powerless, we cannot help ourselves. Your fighting policy will not work down in our section. You dare not come down our way and advocate the doctrine which you preach. You are like the dog that barks and growls only when he is in his master's yard. You can not carry your fighting talk beyond the 'Mason and Dixon Line.' If you are brave enough, and think you can, come down and try it. But don't you think for one moment that we are cowards because we lift our voices protesting in an humble yet sensible way, and get results. For we can, and do, do more of this loud, boastful mandatory talk than you can come down here and do. They understand us, and they would not understand you. And you would not live to return and tell the story of what they did to you and to your Northern brethren, should you come down and make the attempt. Our industrious and diplomatic policy has done and is doing much for us. We are both struggling for the same thing. Our ideas are the same, but our sections of the country and the people who dwell therein demand different methods of procedure, that is all. And the things that you consider hardships, we have found them to be benefits.

"We are none the losers by having separate schools. Thousands and thousands of dollars have found their way into our pockets through the separate school system. Our teaching force is becoming more and more efficient each year, through contact and practice among the youth of the race. They are learning to do by doing. They could never have secured the advantage that they now have here in your section. Besides, it gives to our boys and girls at least one occupation that cannot be called drudgery. Your children of the North finish with honors in the schools and colleges of this section, ofttimes outstripping the Anglo Saxon boy or girl in the attainment of scholarship. And to what purpose, when this coworker, weaker than himself, secures the big paying position and he is forced to take to the fields of drudgery?

"What inducements have your boys and girls to complete a course here in the North? It matters not how well trained or equipped for usefulness that they are, they must leave the Northern fireside and come to this, our Southern clime, if they would practice what they know and receive compensation for what they do.

"Again, mistreatment at the hands of those who run the business in the South, the common grocery clerk and dry goods dealer has caused or forced us to establish business of our own. Dozens of small groceries and notion stores can be found in our segregated districts. Many men of our race are doing things in a business-like way and are supported by the patronage of their own people. Is this not worth while? Is this not asserting manhood? Such enterprise proclaims our dissatisfaction louder and even more forcibly than the harshly spoken words to which are meaningless because they have no power behind them.

"Growth in business and in the world of trade and commerce, and in the industries, is the greatest need of the Negro race. 'Jim Crow Cars' forced segregation and spiteful discrimination are indeed odious and devilish to all intents and purposes, yet they have been and are now the great compelling forces, that have caused the Negro of the South to branch out and try to do something in the way of business for himself and posterity. We have banks and business along nearly all lines. We are wide awake. We are progressing. We are attracting attention. We are gaining respect and recognition. We are giving to the capable boys and girls of our race employment. We are living for posterity. This unjust treatment, this oppression, this humiliation is hammering and chiseling and shaping us into the form of a new and distinct nation, which, in future years, shall receive favors and recognition because of its progress, its merits and its manhood. What results can you show, my Northern brother, by pursuing your revengeful fighting policy? Perhaps you have not gone far enough along that line to attain results. Then continue a little longer, and when you find that you have been forced to yield up your rights and privileges, one by one, that the other race has forced you to let loose entirely the small hold which you have had upon it, then come and join us, not sectionally, but take on our spirit in your own section, and at least make an attempt along business, commercial and professional lines. Don't stand in your own light, fearing to branch out for yourselves lest you should offend the people of your own race by sowing seeds of prejudice and by instituting voluntary segregation. Open up the vast fields of business and trade which are strange and new to Northern colored people. There will be failures, of course, but we must get the drill, we must have the practice. Posterity is dependent upon us, and will profit by our many mistakes. And let us remember that we can learn to do, only by doing."

This is substantially the argument made by all Southern colored people, and this is the argument that Charles Christopher would have made to George Simmons that eventful morning of the fight, had George not lost his temper and so ruthlessly and so grossly insulted him.

But neither the Simmons family or any of the Northern born people were prepared to listen to or heed such advice, coming from the South. They could not and would not accept it. And, granting this, that the Southern people were progressing along business and professional lines; what was that in a country where they have to step aside when they see a white man coming and let him pass; where they have to be bowing and scraping and apologizing all the time, lest they be characterized and considered a saucy "nigger?"

CHAPTER VIII

Reverses For The Simmons Family.

Three years have passed since the first events recorded in our story took place. Many changes have been wrought in this specific northern city, as well as in the lives of our characters who are playing leading roles.

The Simmons family is not what it used to be. Captain Simmons is no longer clerk in the city treasurer's office. "The mills of the Gods grind slowly, but they grind exceedingly fine." Politics and prejudice have at last got in their work, and two years ago Captain Simmons was forced to step down and out from his lucrative position. He tried to shift the blame on the shoulders of the Southern Negro, but the points that he made were so farfetched that his friends were unable to see. Hence, the view that he took was not accepted. He put forth many strenuous efforts to regain what he had lost, but to no avail. So, for two years, he has remained practically idle. He sees the influence that

he once held in the community, and epsecially
among his own people, slipping away.

Money is very scarce with him, and his
creditors are harassing him.   Taxes, insur-
ance, water bills and street improvements
have reduced him.   He is aging rapidly, and
worry is beginning to tell on him.   He is still
hopeful, however, and tries hard, yet, to
brace up and look his friends and foes squarely in the face.   Mrs. Simmons, whose locks
are now silvering, understands her husband
too well.   No counterfeit goes around her.
She knows the real condition, and her husband need not try to fool her or try to hide
from her the financial strait in which he is
entangled.

Yet the good woman knows not what to
do to relieve the strain.   She sees her husband worrying and, of course, she needs must
worry, too.   George is working as porter in
one of the down town stores, but his salary is
not sufficient to meet the demands of the
family, besides George is a good dresser and
struggles hard to keep up appearances.
Naturally proud and ambitious, he often tries
to make his young women friends and associates believe that he is a clerk in the store in
which he works, but they know better because they have seen him at work, and they

think less of him on account of his attempt
to deceive them.

Lillian is as sweet and beautiful as ever.
She has lost none of her charm and grace. A
little more sedate and womanly, perhaps.
But the beautiful glow remains upon her
cheek and the youthful gleam is still in her
eye. She seems to gain in loveliness and at-
traction as the years go by. She takes great
delight in being in mother's and father's company and does much to console them when
they are troubled.

Captain Simmons loves her dearly and
has often been heard to say that he could not
live without her.

Lillian also understands the situation regarding her father's financial condition, and
is anxious to relieve the strain. She is
willing to go out and work in service, but her
beloved parents will not, under any circumstances, hear to it. She knows well how to
do house work and is anxious to put her
knowledge into practice to benefit the family.

"Well, mother, what are we going to
do?" she said one morning at the breakfast
table, after George and her father had left.
"We can't sit here and see the property taken
away from us." Through some chance remark they learned that Captain Simmons
must mortgage his home to meet certain obli-

gations. Mrs. Simmons was heart broken and hot tears were rolling down her cheeks. George and his father could not stand a sight like this, so they had left the table when Lillian confronted her mother with the above question. "I am just going to get out and hunt some work, that's all. I cannot see where the disgrace will come in."

"There is no disgrace in honest labor, my dear, but you have never had to resort to anything like that and such a step would create so much gossip. I don't mind the talk of the ordinary people, but I cannot bear to have those of our set cast insinuations or reflections against us. I can never consent to it, Lillian. I had rather live on bread and water than have you leave home for such a purpose."

"Why, mother," said Lillian, "I did not know that you had so much false pride. I thought that this was why you gave me training in domestic science, you wanted me to be able to earn something, and in case of emergency to be able to take care of myself. You know that there is nothing else that I can do. And I feel so miserable sitting around here idle, a burden on you and papa. I want to help you out."

Mrs. Simmons said not a word. The tears began to flow faster and faster, and

Lillian, seeing that her mother was almost
ready to break down, said in her most cheerful voice, "I tell you, mother, how would it
do for me to advertise as a cateress and
wait parties?"

Mrs. Simmons, not wishing to discourage Lillian, looked up remarking, "I had
never once thought of that, my dear. There
is really a degree of professionalism in that
and I don't know but what it might be a
good thing to do. I might be able to help you
in that. We both could work along together.
It is true we ought to do something to help
father out of this strain. I will speak to him
about it when he returns, and see what he
thinks about it.

CHAPTER IX

A Teacher Wanted

At that moment there was a knock at the door. Lillian rose to open it and, with an exclamation of delight, announced in Bishop Granville, of the A. M. E. church.

Mrs. Simmons, who had not seen the Bishop for a number of years, also expressed her surprise and delight. The three chatted away cheerfully for some time. They seemed to forget all their troubles and worries in the presence of the distinguished divine. They chatted away at length, when finally the Bishop informed them that he must be going. "I am only here," said he "for a few hours. I want to see the pastor of your church on some very important business. By the way, Miss Lillian, I must call you Miss now, you have grown to be such a beautiful young lady, I am on the lookout for a good teacher to teach in a Southern colored school. Do you know any graduates from your High School here that I could recommend for the place? You are a graduate, are you not? Suppose you let me send you down there?

101

What do you say, Madam?" said the Bishop, turning to Mrs. Simmons.

"Oh, mama! do let me go. It is the very thing," exclaimed Lillian, clapping her hands in delight and almost betraying the family troubles by her anxious tone and manner.

"I don't know about that," said Mrs. Simmons, remembering her attitude toward colored schools and colored teachers. "I have always been averse to separate schools and colored teachers, and have several times publicly lifted my voice against them, and it would now seem so inconsistent for me to permit my own daughter to take up a line of work entirely opposite to the principles which I have held, to the doctrine which I have always preached."

"My dear Mrs. Simmons!" exclaimed the Bishop in surprise. "You don't mean to tell me that you oppose separate schools in the South, do you, or in the North, either, as to that matter? Well, my good woman, you are standing in your own light," said the Bishop, somewhat peeved. "Your daughter is missing a great opportunity if you continue to adhere to the stand which you have heretofore taken. Take my advice and cease to advocate doctrine that is not in keeping with the growth and development of the talents

"I have always been averse to colored schools
and colored teachers."

and skill which is dormant in your own race, and in your own children."

Mrs. Simmons listened to what the good man said, very patiently. There was a time when it would be useless for anyone to call her attention to such things as the Bishop had, for she would have turned a deaf ear to him. She made no reply, but stood looking in another direction in a thoughtful manner.

"Come, Sister Simmons, what do you say?" said the Bishop, believing her to be giving the matter favorable consideration.

"Well, Bishop Granville, I will have to think it over. I will talk to Mr. Simmons about it and see what he says. What salary does the position pay?" she asked.

"Well, they pay according to the length of time one serves as a teacher. They begin with sixty-five dollars per month, and after three years they continue to increase until they reach the maximum, which is one hundred dollars per month. This will be a fine thing for Miss Lillian. I want her to see what the South is doing, and this will be her opportunity. The school lasts ten months."

"When will you be back this way?" asked Mrs. Simmons.

"In about three weeks from now. But if you decide to let her go, you had better send word to my next stopping place. I will be there for a week. Here is my address," writing it on a card, he handed it to her. "You see," he continued, "they want to get the matter of selecting teachers out of the way as soon as possible, though school will not open until September. That will give Miss Lillian a chance to prepare."

"I shall depend upon you, child. I know your parents will consent. I shall make no further inquiry for a teacher. I will see that you secure the position." With this he bade them a hearty good-bye and departed for the residence of the minister.

"Mother," said Lillian, after the Bishop had gone, "surely the Lord sent his good Angel to our relief. This is a certain answer to my prayers. Oh, how thankful I am that he came with the offer. Just think, sixty-five dollars per month. In ten months' time I will have enough money to pay off all the debts. Papa can now mortgage the property with safety and secure the ready cash, and relieve the immediate strain, can't he, mamma?"

"Don't be too elated, my dear," said Mrs. Simmons, with a smile. "You are not gone yet. Your father will have to have something to say about it. Besides, I have not wholly made up my mind that that will be the proper thing to do. You know the decided stand that we took three years ago against Jim Crowism."

"Well, I don't care, mother, you all were wrong at that time, anyway. This will be simply an acknowledgment that you were wrong in your opinions regarding separate schools. An open confession will harm no one. Don't be too proud to acknowledge when you are wrong and try to make amends if possible," said Lillian, thinking of Charles Christopher. "Besides," she continued, "these people have nothing to offer us, and when we are down they look upon us with scorn. Look how they did when I attempted to get up a music class. They felt as you have felt, that they must have a white music teacher for their children. And I know that I am better prepared to teach music than the teacher that most of them have secured.

"Away with this false pride and this love for the other race, and the foolish idea that people of our own race have no ability. We can do just as well as any one else, and a great many times better, when we have the training and the chance."

"I am going South and work in the interest of my people, that's what I am going to do. I see plainly that I can never amount to anything up here."

"Well, my dear, 'tis true that there is nothing for you to do up here, and I am sure that you are fitted for the work down there. I suppose separate schools are alright in the South if they secure people who have been trained in the mixed schools of the North, as you have been, to teach them."

"And I think mixed schools in the North would be alright, too, if they would mix the teaching force," said Lillian. "Why, I was a much better scholar than Maggie Armstrong, always made better marks, and many have been the times that I have worked out her algebra problems for her. Now she is teaching, making one hundred and ten dollars per month. And here I am doing nothing. What is the use to excel in school if a person gets no more out of it than I am getting. One night's honor will not last me for a lifetime. I must have something to do. And if the good Bishop will secure the position, I am going South," said Lillian passionately.

"Why, Lillian, I never saw you so wrought up before. Why, I am surprised at you," said her mother. "Calm yourself a little. If you really wish to go South I shall not oppose you. Whatever your father says is alright with me. Sixty-five dollars per month will be a neat little salary for you. I am glad that you are prepared to earn that much.

The only thing is, I dread the gossip that will follow this movement."

"Mother, if these gossipers were paying our debts for us, it would perhaps do for us to listen to them. But they would not give us a penny to save us and they will laugh at us when we are down. I thought you understood them better than that. I did not think you would heed what they would have to say."

At the dinner table Captain Simmons was told of the Bishop's visit, and of his offer to Lillian. Captain Simmons was highly elated over the news, which was especially cheering to him who knew not which way to turn to escape his debtors who were harassing him continually.

"Yes, Lillian, you may go. I am proud of you. Those people down there need more of our intelligent, educated people in their midst. There is a great field of labor in the South."

Mrs. Simmons confronted him with the question of inconsistency. "We, in principle, are opposed to separate schools," said she. "How are we going to harmonize this step with our views?"

"Never mind that, mother," answered Captain Simmons. "Every one up here knows what is the custom down there, and they know that they need the very best talent possible to cope with the ignorance that prevails. Why, many of our Northern white people have gone South to teach colored people. And besides we do not have to tell people what Lillian is doing. If you fear criticism, we will keep her whereabouts a secret."

Lillian did not say very much, although she did not like the idea of keeping the matter secret. But she was too glad to have her father take the stand in her favor, to offer any objections at this time.

George was glad to know that his sister had such an offer, which meant so much in a financial way. He was anxious for the burden of the family support which, at present, was resting heavily on his shoulders, to be lightened some, even by his beautiful beloved sister. He had the same feeling, though, that he would have had if she had been going away as missionary to the heathen land of Africa.

George's ideas and criticism of the Southern people must be overlooked by the reader. For he had never been in that section, nor had he ever met any of the wealthy and highly educated Southern colored people who sometimes visit through the summer in the North. He is young and inexperienced, but he is sensible and can and will be taught better some day.

That night Mrs. Simmons, spurred on by the sensible words, as she thought, spoken by her husband and anxious to relieve the financial strain, eagerly sat down and wrote Bishop Granville a letter thanking him for his kind suggestions and the interest he had taken in her daughter. That after looking into the matter of which he spoke, she and her husband, Captain Simmons, had decided to allow their daughter Lillian to take the position as teacher in the South. Fearing that there might be some slip, she urged the Bishop to be sure and do all that he could. Now that she had decided, she did not want anything to go wrong. That if anything should happen to prevent Lillian's securing the position, the disappointment to the family would be great. She closed her letter in the customary way, sealed it and sent it away that same night by special delivery.

The next day she received the reply. The Bishop was very glad that she had set aside the prejudice which she had always held against colored schools and teachers and told her so in his letter. He told her to have no fear, that the place was secure for Lillian. And thanked her and Mr. Simmons for reaching the right conclusion and for so promptly informing him. He closed invoking the richest blessings from Heaven upon the whole family.

CHAPTER X

A BUSINESS VENTURE

In the past three years Charles Christopher has visited many places in the North. He has had an opportunity to observe many things and has not failed to make note of them. At the various summer resorts where he has been employed he has been in close contact with all classes of people and has made them a study. Sociology, psychology and other subjects along the lines of human interest naturally appeal to him. He is also a constant visitor to the Library and has devoured the contents of many books. Besides, he reads the daily papers and is up on all the current news of the days. Broad minded, big hearted, he grows in gentility, dignity and manhood as the years go by.

He often thinks of Lillian Simmons and has an overwhelming desire to see her once more. He has been tempted many times to write her, just to send her a post card, but each time his heart has failed him. He realizes full well the truth of the oft repeated expression, "A faint heart never won fair

112

lady," but he has not the courage to drop the many letters that he has nerved himself to write to her, in the mail box. He is strong and courageous in all things else, seemingly, except in friendly overtures and courtship to beautiful Lillian Simmons. He cannot rely upon the hope which she held out to him, as a reward for the sacrifice that he made to please or to gratify her, the day on which he left. He is afraid that he may have misunderstood, that her tone and manner did not bespeak what he at first had hoped. It was very possible that he, being excited and carried away by her abrupt appearance, was mistaken, after all. Besides, he had neglected so long that it was no use to try to gain recognition from her now. "If she is not married to another she has forgotten me in this time," he thought. Thus, for a long time, he would think of her and wonder if he would ever see her again.

Time rolled on and Charles continued to work. It is now the month of September. Charles has saved up a good sized bank account and he is anxious to go into business for himself. Being familiar with the grocery business he begins to think out some locality that would be suitable for a business venture along this line. And, after running over the list of cities and towns in which he had been, and having made notes of the possibilities for a business venture among colored people in them, he decided that there would be no better place to start than in the town where he had met opposition because he was from the South.

There was at least three thousand colored people in the place, the majority of whom lived well and owned their own homes. He could see no reason why they would not trade with him. He would keep a neat, clean place and though his stock would be small, it should be as good and as fresh as any.

He had also noticed that the white people of the North were indeed very friendly and were disposed to recognize the true worth of a man, and he felt sure that many of them would trade with him if he should carry such things as they would want.

He is ready to acknowledge that there is a much better spirit existing toward colored people, as a race, in the North than there is in the South. The Southern white people bestow their love and friendship upon individuals of the race on account of family ties and past remembrances of loyalty and other sentimental reasons. But they care naught for them as a race. They can see nothing in them. They criticize them for being rough,

uncouth and shiftless, without thinking of
the original cause of their degradation.

The Northern white people have a tendency to look upon them with pity and are
really glad to see them prosper. And Charles
Christopher, ever on the alert, was sensible
to this fact, and was always ready to thank
them and to show his appreciation. Although
it was not pity that he wanted, but a fair
chance, and he would do the rest.

He went over his plans several times in
his mind and finally, concluding that he was
on the right road, decided that he would quit
the place where he was now working in about
ten days and start for the scene of his
venture.

Charles was a young man of decision,
and when he made up his mind to do a thing
he would, as a rule, go through with it. So,
upon the day set, he departed for the city
where he had been the cause of so much
turmoil and strife. For even after he was
gone from the place it seemed that outbreaks
and disturbances were more frequent than
ever, due to the Northern people tightening
up reins, so to speak, and attempting to re-
strain the Southern people from utterances
which did not harmonize with their own, and
the Southern people's resistance, who it
seemed had become emboldened, partly by the

remarks of the paper and partly by old man Littlejohn's speech and the stand which he took in their behalf at the meeting that night. They began to think and talk among themselves after that. They were not long in discovering that they were in the majority, and they knew that they were free and did not have to be afraid to express their views along the lines of their policy, for the solution of the race problem. All this caused the confusion among the people.

But since Captain Simmons has lost his position, and with it the greater part of his influence, things have been much quieter. He and his son, George, and Frank Maxwell, were the chief agitators, but now it seems that they have no following and it is difficult for them to get a hearing.

So there is no better time for Charles Christopher to begin business in that city than now. He boards the train and is soon speeding, at a rapid rate, toward the place of destiny. Enchanted by the beautiful scenes along the route, Charles falls into day dreaming. He pulls back the curtain and takes a peep into the dim future. He beholds himself a man of wealth and influence, engaged in mercantile pursuits and owner of large business interests. He sees a fickle populace courting favors at his hands. He sees himself a stalwart leader of his people, shielding them from the wiles of the demagogue and the snares of the unscrupulous politicians. He hears himself preaching the doctrines of love and truth. He warns against the vice and the shame and pretense in society. He sees himself first a true friend, then a lover of Lillian Simmons. He hears the chimes of the wedding bells. He sees himself a trusted husband and then a doting father. And then, by a sudden lurch of the train, he awakes from his reverie and finds himself the same simple, plain, yet sensible, Charles Christopher that he has always been.

The train having entered the city, his trained eye catches glimpses of the familiar sights as it glides swiftly along. Here flows the Majestic river. There, upon its banks, is the same rustic bench upon which he sat in reverie the morning when Lillian Simmons approached, fairylike, and pleaded with him to leave the city. There is the spot where he and George Simmons, like gladiators, fought. Over yonder is the Simmons' stately, but somewhat weatherbeaten home. It is badly in need of paint.

The train is now at the depot from which he departed three years ago. He realizes more fully, now, where he is and what is his purpose. He wonders if Lillian Simmons is still in the city, and will he have a chance to see her. He picked up his grip and moved slowly toward the door of the crowded train. And as he was descending the steps, lifting his eyes, he beheld, gazing into his face, the heavy lashed, deeply set black eyes of Lillian Simmons. Amid the shouts of "Good-bye" and waving hands, Lillian Simmons got on the train that Charles Christopher got off. It was all like a dream to both of them, so quickly did it happen. A glance, a recognition and a deep thrill of the heart and that was all!

Charles Christopher had come and Lillian Simmons had gone, and not a word was spoken. So a great barrier still exists between these two who would be friends. "The irony of fate," thought Charles, as he stood and watched the train, with increasing speed, move away, bearing Lillian Simmons thither he knew not where. Then, collecting himself with an effort, he boarded a car and rode up into the city.

The whole Simmons family and many of their friends were at the station to see Lillian off. They saw Charles, when he alighted from the train, and were too surprised, at first, to say anything. George finally whispered to his mother and told her that old Charley Christopher had gotten off the train.

"Is that so," said Mrs. Simmons, "where is he? I have never seen him."

"There he is, getting on the car," said George.

"Is that he? Why, I never figured his being that sort of a looking fellow. He is not a rough looking man, at all. I wonder why he comes back here," said Mrs. Simomns.

"I don't have the least idea," said George. "I know this, though, he shall not stay here long." He then turned to his father, who was a few steps behind, and said: "Father, I guess we will have to call another meeting. I see that Charley Christopher is back here."

"Who is Charley Christopher?" returned his father.

"Why, surely you haven't forgotten him. He is the Southern darky that I had the fight with three years ago. You know, the one we ran away from here," said George, sneeringly.

"Oh, yes," said his father. "Was that him who got off the train?"

"Yes," replied George.

"Well, wait," said Captain Simmons. I thought I had seen that face before. I wonder what he wants here, now."

"I have not the least idea," said George. "Don't you think we had better get the boys together and find out?"

"Well, wait a day or two. Maybe he means no harm. We will not molest him as long as he behaves himself."

"Alright," said George, turning to go to his work, which was in a different direction to that his parents had to go.

Mr. and Mrs. Simmons were too deeply engrossed in the welfare of their daughter Lillian to allow the subject of Charles Christopher's return to the city to find lodgment in their minds. So no more was said about it at that time.

Charles Christopher wasted no time after his arrival in the city. He set out at once in search of a desirable locality in which to begin his new venture. Of course, he had no thought of finding a place way down in the heart of the city, for there the rent would be too high. What he wanted was a place in a colored locality, so near that they would prefer to trade with him rather than go a long distance to town for the small things in the grocery line which are very often needed in a rush. He was not long in finding the place that suited him. About ten squares from the main part of the city and remote from any car line, and at the entrance of a colored settlement, he located his neat little grocery store. His stock, though small, was complete. Tastily arranged and fresh in appearance. It was not long before the people were tempted to buy. The first day after opening he counted his customers. Twenty white and fourteen colored persons had been in and made small purchases. After the first week he was, by his increasing trade, assured of great success. Many words of encouragement fell from the lips of the people who welcomed his enterprise. They found it to their interest to have him in their midst, and felt that he was accommodating them by locating near them. And, too, he was so kind and obliging. His personality, which he had seized the opportunity to develop when traveling when employed in the various hotels of the North, was now asserting itself, for through it he was enabled to handle his patrons successfully and increase his trade.

Say what you will, it is the man with the vim and with a pleasing personality who gets the big business. In six months' time Charles was enabled to double his stock and his prospects for future business and trade had increased a hundred per cent. Much comment was made on his enterprise, and words of praise could be heard for him on every hand. The colored people had begun to feel proud of their colored store. "Christopher's Grocery" was all the talk among them. They took great pride in telling strangers about it and each one felt, somehow, that he had an interest in it. Every one was pleased except Frank Maxwell and the Simmons family.

CHAPTER XI

MRS. SIMMONS' REBUKE

George Simmons watched the business grow and listened to the praise bestowed upon Charles Christopher with disgust. He was intensely human and could not help feeling keenly the pangs of jealousy and envy caused by the progress and popularity of his erstwhile foe. And in an intensely human way he began to plan an interruption, to impede, if possible, to stay Charles Christopher's rapid growth.

Captain Simmons felt piqued at the way the people were supporting a Negro business, and could have and would have taken some steps to stop it if there had not been so many white people trading there, also. He could not argue that Negroes were separating themselves from the whites, that they were sowing seeds of prejudice, that they were endorsing and inviting segregation. The bottom had fallen out of his argument, since the whites were praising Charles so highly and were encouraging him with their patronage. So he was at a loss. He could think of nothing to say or do.

Lillian's having to go South to teach, and Charles Christopher's coming North and entering into a successful business, set Mrs. Simmons to thinking deeply regarding the race problem. She often thought of the words of Bishop Granville the morning when he made the offer for Lillian to teach in the South. "Cease to advocate doctrine that is not in keeping with the growth and development of the talents and skill which is dormant in your own race and in your own children." His words then had the ring of truth about them and she had often dwelt upon them.

And now they have more meaning in them when she notes the success that Charles Christopher is having, through his business enterprise. She, too, in a way, envies him. Like all good mothers, she would be so glad were it her son. She now sees clearly which boy has the better chance. She realizes that the man doing business for himself has a great advantage over the one working for some one else. How grand it would have been had she and Captain Simmons, while in a prosperous condition, had had the good sense to have started some kind of business for themselves. They would have been independent by now, and could be able to give their own children employment. "But it is too late, now," she thought. "I can't see how George can ever be anything else other than a porter in a dry goods store where he is now working. He doesn't make enough money to lay any of it away. If Mr. Simmons don't get something to do soon, I don't know what will become of us. Perhaps the Negroes of the South are right, after all, in pursuing their policies advocating separate business and separate schools. I see plainly the advantage of both."

That evening at the supper table Charles Christopher was the subject of discussion by the Simmons family.

Mrs. Simmons began by asking George what purpose had he in life. She could see nothing for him, but she thought perhaps he had some plan that he had never unfolded to herself and Mr. Simmons. He was now past twenty-five and she thought it time for him to make up his mind what he would like to do.

Charles Christopher's success had brought things to an issue. His Southern idea looked good to her, and she wanted to find out what George thought about it.

"Do you always expect to remain a porter in the dry goods store?" said she, putting the question directly.

"Why, no, mother," said George, in an injured tone.

"Well, what do you purpose to take up as a life work?" she asked.

George sat silent. He really had no purpose. He had gotten past the place where he was so ambitious. In the past year or so he seemed content to draw his small weekly pittance and have it spent almost before it was made. 'Tis true he had used most of it at home while the family was in such straitened circumstances, still he realized that he was not making the headway that he should, considering his superior education and training. But he knew nothing else that he could do, so he was simply drifting, he knew not where.

"Tell me what you are going to do, George," insisted his mother.

It was plain that George had no definite aim or plan in life and his mother felt sorry for him. She felt that she and her husband was the cause of his destitution of ideas. She began to think what the other race has provided for their children. They have factories, foundries, stores and business of all sorts in which to place them. Whether they finish school or not, they can find employment for them.

But what have the colored people for their children to do? Here is George, who is an accomplished scholar, who graduated with high honors and who is as capable as any white boy in the city. What has he to do? He cannot teach, for they do not employ colored teachers in mixed schools. He has applied ofttimes for a position as clerk in the stores, in the shipping houses and in the city hall, but each time he has met with refusal. To get the position as a porter, which he now holds, he had to go through a lot of "red tape," and had to have a tremendous "pull."

"And this is the condition that confronts all young and deserving colored men of the North," thought Mrs. Simmons.

George stammered out some sort of a weak reply to his mother. He said something about becoming a civil engineer, or he would like to take a course in pharmacy. His replies were altogether unsatisfactory to his mother.

"Well," said Mrs. Simmons, "until you and your father show me differently, I am a convert to the Southern idea. I have been watching this fellow Christopher in business and to my way of thinking he was right at the time you all had the fight, and from all appearances he is right now. Things are as plain to me now as they can be. Our family is being benefitted by separate schools, and I am sure it would be greatly benefitted now if we had such a business as Charles Christopher has established. You had just as well have had a business of your own as for Christopher to come here and set up one. I understand that he is getting rich. It is so strange that we have all been so blind. As I say, if I am wrong, I want you and your father to set me right. How about it, Mr. Simmons?"

Captain Simmons had been sitting listening quietly to what Mrs. Simmons was saying. He realized that much of what she said was true. But he was not frank enough to admit it. He said that Mrs. Simmons could think as she pleased, but as for him, he never would become a believer in Southern Negro ideas. And as for Charles Christopher, he bet he would go under in a short time. As all other Negro undertakings usually do.

"But you will admit," returned Mrs. Simmons, "that we would be better off if George had a business like that, will you not? I have never been there, but they say his place is always full and that he has as much white trade as colored. He is kept busy all the time."

"That's alright, mother. He will go under, just the same. Then you will have a chance to try your hand. If you think you have enough business ability, I will see if I can't start you off."

Seeing that he would be unable to carry on a successful argument with his wife, this was the joking way in which Captain Simmons turned her aside.

"Well," said Mrs. Simmons, "I am serious about it. I do wish that George did have some kind of business of his own."

George had nothing more to say.

CHAPTER XII

CHRISTOPHER'S GROCERY BURNS

At the mention of Charles Christopher
the pangs of envy and jealousy began to gnaw
at George's heart. "He is showing me up, is
he?" was the thought that entered his mind.
"I guess he is here to try to prove his side of
the argument. He wants to make his Southern ideas stick, I guess. Alright. We'll see."

Supper now being over they arose and
left the table. George put on his hat and coat
and went toward town.

That night about twelve o'clock the hid-
eous sound of the city fire alarm broke the
stillness of the night. Shouts of fire were
distinctly heard in the Southeast section of
the city. The colored people were greatly
excited. "Fi—er! Fi—er!! was heard in all
directions.

Soon the clatter of hoofs and the clang-
ing of bells were heard distinctly for blocks
away. And in less time than it takes to tell
it, the beautiful panting animals were reined
up champing their bits in the vicinity of
Charles Christopher's grocery store, which

Charles Christopher's Grocery Store Was in
Flames.

was in flames. No one knew how long the building had been burning before the alarm was turned in, but it was evident to the fire chief that it could not be saved, so he simply let it burn and sent his men to the task of saving other buildings which were near and were in imminent danger.

When Charles Christopher came upon the scene, he staggered and almost fell at the sight of his hard earned savings curling heavenward in a dense cloud of smoke, the accumulations of several toilsome years ruthlessly snatched from his hands. The object wherein lay his fondest future dreams, transformed as it were, into naught. None except he who has gone through a similar experience can sympathize fully with Charles Christopher, or understand why he sat down on a nearby stone and, strong man that he was, wept like a child. He knew nothing else to do. He felt that he was done for, for all time. To struggle up the rugged hills of life again to where he now was, would be too hard and would take too long. He had not the courage nor strength to try. All his future hopes and happiness were now smouldering in ashes.

How did it happen? This question was everywhere asked. If the reader has not already guessed aright we know that it would interest him also to know. But as some investigations must be made, and as such should not be done in haste, we will for the time turn our attention to Lillian Simmons, of whom we have not heard for some time, and in whom we know our readers have as much interest as they have in the immediate fire mystery.

CHAPTER XIII

A Colored Town

B—— is a beautiful little town of the South with an entire colored population, situated in the midst of a rich farming district that feeds fat off the wheat and corn, and cattle and milk, produced by the farmers and brought to market within its limits. On Saturdays its streets are thronged with sober, business-like people, selling their wares and making needful purchases from its well stocked stores. It is really inspiring to see how these people, as if by instinct, take to trade and barter and have thus become a part of the commercial world. Drummers representing the great wholesale houses of the country, make regular visits to this enterprising and fast growing little city of five thousand inhabitants of colored people. It has all the attributes necessary for a great and thriving town.

Everything is as it should be, and the persons who have striven to build it deserve credit. Its schools and churches are of a high standard and are well equipped, with men

135

and women of good character and excellent educational qualifications. And if the colored people of the North could visit it and note the clock-like precision with which the wheels of industry turn, note the poise, the ease, the confidence, with which the people carry on their operations, note the good will and harmony which prevails among them, they would then have more respect for the colored South, they would view life in a different light and all doubts as to a happy future for the Negro race would be dispelled. One can be benefitted in a hundred different ways by visiting this town.

It was in this Utopian city with its people of varied hues, that Lillian Simmons, after four days of tiresome travel, found herself. When she alighted at the station she found the ticket agent, the baggage master and the operator, all colored. She went up town and to the Post Office and found the Postmaster and his five or six assistants colored. She found the Mayor and all the city officers colored. The four or five blocks of business in the city were under the control of colored people. Grocery stores, dry goods stores, feed stores, shoe stores, drug stores, furniture stores, candy stores, meat shops, restaurants, fruit stands and all of the various lines of trade, were managed by persons

of African descent.   Three cotton gins, a
livery stable and a lumber yard, she learned,
were successfully run by colored men.   The
streets were paved and the city was well
lighted by an electric plant owned by a
wealthy Negro, who had secured the services
of a colored electrician.   The dwellers in this
unique, but beautiful little city, were all
colored.   The pale faces of the other race
could not be seen here.   And Lillian's heart
swelled with pride when she alighted from
the train and looked, for the first time, upon
her new field of labor and saw the makeup of
its citizenry.   A new feeling came over her.
Lillian Simmons was no "put on," but under
these new and strange, yet happy and inspiring environments, she could not help assuming the air and carriage of a Queen.   She
felt so safe, so secure, where her own people,
with the wisdom of the ancient romans, were
reigning supreme.   To say that she was
amazed and carried away at what she saw is
putting it too mildly.   She was astounded.
In her wildest dreams she had never fancied
that there was such a place under the sun
as this for her people.   "If George and
mama and papa could only see this," she
thought.

CHAPTER XIV

The Jim Crow Car

On her way down South, after reaching that section where she was asked to take a seat in the cars prepared for colored passengers, Lillian's heart sank within her. She had often heard about it, but she had never known what real humiliation was until she was asked by the conductor to take her baggage and go into the next car where she could see plainly in bold black type, a placard in the far end of the coach, "This car for Negroes." She began to wish that she had not come to a country so heartless, so void of justice, so full of—not prejudice, but pure meanness, as to force a hardship like this on a decent, cultured woman who was traveling alone.

The coach into which she had to go was really filthy. The seats were cushionless and very uncomfortable, being of the old cane bottom kind. At each station disrespectful loud-mouthed foolish Negroes were getting on and off. She was perfectly disgusted with the side of Negro life in the South which she saw on the train and from the car window. She was satisfied, now, that her father and mother and George were right in their fight against the influx of Southern Negroes into the North. She almost cried when one vile, uncouth idiot of a Negro, who was riding backwards so he could look her squarely in the face, shouted to her, "Hello pitty yaller gal, where is you goin?" O, how she wished for her big hot-headed brother, George. But the ugly Negro said no more. He simply sat gazing at her. Lillian began to wonder if the South were not really justified in lynching such depraved animals as the fellow showed himself to be. He was so impudent with the brim of his dusty cap pulled to one side, his shirt opened at the neck, exposing an old knit undergarment, black with dirt. She saw many such types before the completion of her journey. In fact she saw enough to put her out with Southern Negroes forever. She could understand why "Jim Crow cars" and all other forms of segregation in the South were necessary, but she could not feel that it was fair to treat all colored people alike, because all were not alike.

After she had ridden in the separate coach for some time and had become somewhat reconciled to the condition, the conductor, who was apparently waiting for this moment, approached her in a friendly way and asked her where she was going and where she was from. She told him, and she could scarcely keep back the tears, for she felt that he was sympathizing with her.

"Yes, I thought so," said he. "I am very sorry, indeed, to place you in here, but you know we have to obey the law," he said with a sorrowful smile.

"I guess you are right," said Lillian.

"Well, cheer up, little girl. I will see that no harm comes to you. Have any of these fellows been annoying you?"

"Yes," she said, "that fellow sitting with his face this way, called to me insultingly when he first got on the train. You can see how impudently he stares at me."

"That fellow right there?" said the conductor.

"Yes," replied Lillian.

The conductor went to him and informed him that he would be put off if he said another word to the lady. He was told to sit face front, anyway, in the car. The Negro readily obeyed the conductor in his authoritative tone and look, and Lillian had no further trouble with him.

She began, after that, to think of the sacrifice of pleasure and privileges that she was making in the interest of the family.

This thought alone consoled her. She was glad to do so. She would not murmur; she would put up with whatever should come to her. "Maybe all the people of the South are not like those that I have seen. There may be some more like Charles Christopher," she thought. "But not just like him," she changed, remembering her affection for him. "I wonder what he is going to do. I am satisfied that he knew me when he got off the train. Oh, I am so sorry that I was leaving just as he arrived. I did not even get to speak to him. I believe I will write to him," she said to herself.

She was now nearing her destination. And lo and behold, when she alighted from the train and saw the sights as told above, the bad impression of the South that she had received through the restless, unsettled, thoughtless, depraved actions of a certain floating element passed swiftly from her mind, to be remembered against it no more. And she wished that mama and papa and George could see what she now so gloriously beheld. "I know that I shall be happy if this is to be my environment," she thought.

She was soon settled in her new home which was with the Principal of the school and his charming wife. The Bishop had secured a good boarding place for her as well as the position as teacher.

Lillian was a successful teacher and it is needless for us to go through the details of relating her experience as such. Suffice it to say that she won the love and friendship of pupils and parent, which is the first and last requisite of success in a colored school. She was always busy in some needful way. Besides being an indispensable worker in the school room, she was a leader in the Literary Society, the Church and the Sunday School. Bright, witty, jovial and intelligent, she made many friends. No social function was a success without her presence. It seemed that she had found her niche, and she was now filling it to perfection.

She would often receive letters from home, and she was so pleased to know of the colored grocery store that had been established by Charles Christopher. And she would often picture herself at home keeping company with the young proprietor of the new grocery store.

CHAPTER XVI

LOVE LETTERS

Once she received a letter from her mother stating that Mabel Lester was making eyes at Charles Christopher, which made poor Lillian very unhappy at the time.

"I am not going to stand for it," she pouted. "He is mine and now I don't care how it looks, I am going to write him." And she did. She went up town and picked out a modest, yet appropriate post card and sent it to him. But had it been possible, after it was in the mail box, for her to have taken it out, she would have done so. But it was too late, now. It went direct and Charles Christopher received it the very next morning after the disastrous fire. Had he not received this card from the beautiful Lillian Simmons, whom he loved so well, dark indeed would have been the days immediately following the unfortunate fire. This card alone gave him strength and courage to bear up. He was willing to try to pull up the rugged hill again for her dear sake.

In return, Charles immediately sat down and wrote Lillian the most beautifully worded letter she had ever received in her life. He told her of his great grief and misfortune and of the hard struggle that he had in reaching the place from which he had so recently been cast down. "But your dear post card came just at the time when I was at my weakest and needed something to strengthen me. You have saved me, my dear friend, from a horrrible fate. I was in great despair and was at the point where I was about to do something desperate," said he in his letter. "But your sweet missive has brought sunshine to me again, and today I feel that after all, life is worth living. I shall not hesitate to try to climb back and even past the height from which I was so suddenly hurled a night ago. Your token of respect and esteem has given me courage and renewed vigor. I thank you from the depths of my heart. Let me hear from you again soon.

"Yours sincerely, Charles Christopher."

Two days later, when Lillian went to the Post Office and received a letter from her home, written in a strange hand, her heart beat faster and her countenance lit up with expectancy. She could hardly take time to open it. Yes, it was from Charles Christopher. "Let's see what he says," she said in

an undertone. She began reading and was
struck dumb when she heard of the great
disaster, the hopes of Charles Christopher
being crumbled into ashes. She read the
part over again and continuing to the end,
she found this one of the saddest, at the same
time, one of the sweetest letters that she
had ever received. She now felt glad that
she had sent the card, that herself and not
Mabel Lester, had the power to cheer him
and help him to bear up under his great
misfortune. She then gave herself over to
thoughts of true love and sympathy for him
and even wished that he was near that she
might lay a tender hand upon his brow and
whisper sweet consoling words to him.

"What caused the fire," she wondered.
Could any one have been so mean, so low, so
void of principle, as to have applied the torch
to his business because it was prosperous?
'Tis true that Charles Christopher had some
bitter enemies. Could some of them have
been mean enough to commit this dastardly
act. No, her brother would not do a thing
like that. She could not for a moment entertain the thought that George would stoop so
low.

She read the letter over several times
that night and she could not bear the idea of
retiring before answering it. It was so sad

and sweet she felt that she could not do it justice, but at any rate she was going to try.

When she had finished writing it was more than an hour after her regular time for retiring. But she was satisfied. She had told him many things that she wished him to know and had all but confessed her love for him. She even made mention of Miss Mabel Lester in a way that indicated that she was greatly concerned and told him not to get too deeply entangled; that she would be home soon.

She concluded her letter with her very best wishes and a hope that the culprit, if such there was, who applied the torch and caused him so much grief and so much loss, would soon be run to ground. With a "Sincerely yours, Lillian Simmons," she closed her letter, sealed it and laid it away to be mailed the next morning.

She retired, but could not rest. "That is a little too bold of me," she thought. "I shall not send it. The idea of my twitting him about Mae Lester. Why, he will think I am silly. Besides he has no time for foolishness like that now. Why, the man is too grieved and worried to think about girls. No, indeed, I shall not send that letter. I will tear it up in the morning and write one with more sense and dignity." Thus musing she soon fell asleep.

Being tired and worried from the late hours spent in writing the night previous, Lillian slept later than usual the next morning.

She finally arose, dressed and went into breakfast. Principal McVain, who had finished his breakfast, was just leaving the dining room. He went out into the hall to get his hat and, glancing into Lillian's room, saw the letter there ready to be mailed, and as was his custom, he went into the room and picked it up and left the house. He proceeded to the school building, and upon arriving he called one of the boys to him and, along with some other mail which he had, sent Lillian's letter to the Post Office. And when Lillian realized what had been done, the unsatisfactory letter, the bold, silly letter was away beyond recall. Lillian cried but it was no use, the letter was gone.

Charles Christopher received it in due time and would have been infinitely happy had not the culprit who applied the torch to his prosperous business been discovered and proved to be the brother of the beautiful sympathetic girl, who had written this love-inspired epistle. She had hoped that the culprit would soon be run to earth, but little did she think that her beloved brother George would be the guilty one. But facts are facts, and as objectionable as they may seem, we are now confronted with them and must deal with them fairly and impartially. George Simmons, upon investigation, was found to have been the one who committed the deed.

CHAPTER XVII

George Simmons' Arrest

Charles Christopher's Grocery Store was situated on a corner and faced but one way. It was a two story building which was twenty-five feet wide and extended back about forty feet on a lot which was a hundred feet deep. On the other end of the lot was a dwelling house which was occupied by a white family. This house was removed from the store building not more than twenty-five or thirty feet. Beneath the store was a cellar, the entrance of which was but a few feet to the left of the back door of the store. The lady who occupied the cottage back of the store testified that she was at her window at eleven thirty o'clock, and saw a man go in the cellar. She paid no special attention to him, because she thought it was Christopher himself going in there for some purpose or other. She had often seen him go in the cellar, but never so late as that. She stated that she was watching for her husband who usually arrived from work about that time. She finally saw the man come out and instead of going into the

149

store, he hastened around to the back of her house. She was not sure whether he went up the alley or not. At any rate, in about a half hour it seemed to her the store was in flames.

The woman's husband testified that he passed the front door of Christopher's store at eleven o'clock and everything was alright. He was on his way home from work, but just as he was entering the door of his home ne saw a man coming out of the cellar of the store. Upon seeing him, the man went back of the house and began running up the alley. Not wishing to create an excitement at that hour of the night, he simply stood at the mouth of the alley and watched the man until he emerged into the street at the other end.

Patrolman McGinty testified that about eleven fifteen o'clock, he was passing along and a man ran out of the alley almost into his arms. He stopped him and asked him where he had been, at that moment he recognized him as George Simmons. "Why, hello, George, it's you is it," said I. "Where have you been, you are off your beat ar'nt you?" He said something about having been to see a friend and was out a little later than usual. I said no more and he walked hurriedly away.

"Are you sure that it was George Simmons?" asked the chief.

"Yes," replied McGinty.

"Well, you had better go and get him and bring him here," said the chief. "He will have to give an account of himself."

George was sitting at the breakfast table discussing the fire with his mother, when a knock was heard at the door. It was about nine o'clock in the morning. It was at this hour that George always got off from work to eat breakfast. Captain Simmons was out at the time. So Mrs. Simmons opened the door. Two policemen pushed themselves past Mrs. Simmons into the room, one of them asking gruffly, "Is George Simmons here?"

"He is," answered Mrs. Simmons.

"Where is he? We have a writ for him."

"A writ for what?" cried Mrs. Simmons. "What has he done?"

"Well he is charged with incendiarism. It is alleged that he set fire to Christopher's grocery store last night, and we have come to arrest him," said one of the officers.

Mrs. Simmons swooned, but George was at her side and caught her in his arms, preventing her from falling to the floor. "Dash a cup of water in her face," said one of the policemen. "That will bring her around alright."

George lay his mother on the couch and going to the hydrant quickly drew a cup of water and dipping his fingers in it, sprinkled some in her face and also bathed her temples. She soon revived, but was too weak or frightened to sit up or to speak. It was really pitiful to see the poor woman so overcome with grief.

At this moment Captain Simmons, who at a distance saw the policemen coming to his house, entered, inquiring what the trouble was.

The officers, knowing Captain Simmons well, having for a number of years associated with him in the city service, called him to one side and explained to him in an undertone the purpose of their visit.

Captain Simmons did not believe that George committed the crime, and begged the men not to arrest him. But his pleadings were of no avail. They told Captain Simmons that they were compelled to do their duty.

They took George before a justice for a preliminary hearing after which he was released on bond, his employers going his security.

The news that George Simmons had set fire to Charles Christopher's store soon spread throughout the city. The papers spoke of it in the most drastic terms and suggested that the culprit suffer the severest punishment at the hands of the law.

Frank Maxwell went to Captain Simmons and told him that the case looked bad for George and thought that the best thing he could do would be to plead guilty and trust himself to the mercy of the court. Captain Simmons would not hear to this. He did not believe his son was guilty, and he would spend every dollar he was worth in the effort to free him.

It is well known to the reader that Captain Simmons is already deeply in debt and this recent trouble only makes matters a whole lot worse than they were. He not having ready cash, places his home under a second heavy mortgage. Mrs. Simmons believing that some hateful conspiracy is being practiced against her son agrees to the transaction of her husband. She had rather be a beggar in the street than have her son behind prison bars when he is innocent. She does not wish to tell Lillian for she knows it will break her heart. But after considering the wisdom of such a step she decides to do so.

So that very night she sat down to break the news to her daughter. She wrote quite a lengthy letter, telling her about the fire, and how certain enemies had plotted to lay the charge at her brother George's door.

"The trial is set a month off so I guess you will be home by that time," she added. "I would not worry your mind with it at all, dear, but you no doubt will hear it any way and it is best that it come to you straight and from the pen of your own mother. We need have no fear from him for his employers are backing him. They went his bond which was fixed at two thousand dollars.

"Father has secured some more money on the place and has employed one of the best lawyers in the city who will fight to the last ditch for us. Frank Maxwell advises George to plead guilty, and perhaps on his record as a good citizen, he will get off with a light jail sentence. But we will not hear to that. 'Tis true that Maxwell is our friend and a lawyer, but he does not know everything."

Mrs. Simmons did not tell Lillian of the damaging evidence against George. She placed as hopeful a construction on the unfortunate situation as possible. She then concluded her letter, sealed it up and spent the rest of the night in grief and tears. Captain Simmons' words of consolation did not do much toward allaying her suffering.

George, after such a trying ordeal as he had gone through, could not look his mother and father in the face. His guilty conscience was playing havoc with his heretofore bold

front and independent air. His countenance
was downcast. 'Twas plain that he felt keenly the disgrace that he had brought to the
family.

Charles Christopher regretted very much
to learn that it was George Simmons who
had destroyed his business. He knew that
George was his enemy, but he had really
placed him away above such an unprincipled
act. He thought that he was a man. Though
they had differed in opinions, Charles respected him and admired him on account of
his fight for a principle. He hated to see him
fall and grovel, as he now was in the dust
with the lowest of criminals, a common of-
fender of the law.

Then too he loved his beautiful sister
and had just began to make headway along
the lines of friendship. He knew keenly Lillian would feel the disgrace, and feared that
her shame and chagrin might be so great that
she would never write him or look him in
the face again. What could he do to lessen
the great embarrassment that he knew she
must feel. This was one of the uppermost
questions in his mind. As to the re-estab-
lishment of himself in business, this was
practically settled. He had sufficient backing for that. Dover the hotel man, Willard
the News reporter and a number of other in-

fluential men in consultation had agreed to assist him and put him on his feet again. He was very much elated over his future business prospects, but to retain the place that he now holds or that he once held in Lillian's affections is the thing that bothers him most.

He resolves however to answer her sweet letter avoiding the mention of the culprit. "But she is certain to know about it anyway," thought he. "Why not just tell her the plain truth? If she is the sensible girl that I take her to be she will think more of me. She will admire me for being frank and fair. Then, too, I will be in a better position to sympathize with her and perhaps lend some assistance. She will feel like taking me into confidence. I think I can do a great deal toward getting George out of this and I am going to write to her and tell her so."

So Charles sat down to the task of answering Lillian's letter which brought so much cheer and happiness, at the same time embarrassment to him the early part of the morning. Among other things he wrote:

"I know George to be my enemy and after looking into the matter I can understand why he resorted to such an awful revenge. At heart I think your brother a good fellow, but he yielded to a thirst for revenge which seems to be a weakness with him, it is in his nature; but in this case were it to do over, I am sure he would not attempt it.

"I am willing to use my influence with my friends to help him out of trouble. And I have a two fold reason for doing so. First I hate to see the best people of our race fall on account of some overt act or thoughtless deed. Your brother did not think of the enormity of the crime until it was committed.

"And I am quite sure that he has repented by now.

"For this reason I shall not appear against him, nor would I under similar conditions appear against any member of my race. I want at all times to be broad and considerate in the treatment of others and especially those of my own people.

"And another reason and perhaps my strongest one, is that I love and respect you my dear one. I would do anything in my power for your happiness. When my heart was heavy and my mind was in the deepest distress, you were so kind and sympathetic to me. So now in this trouble I want your full confidence. I want to befriend you. Ask what you will of me, and if it is in my power to grant it, it shall be done."

He closed his letter by thanking her for the kind words of consolation that she had

written him and promised that he would not
be entangled with Mae Lester to any great
extent when she returned. He simply
thought well of Mabel as a friend and nothing more. That he would be only too glad to
be her constant company and escort on all
occasions when she returned if she would
permit.

With sincere love and respect he closed
the letter and mailed it to Lillian Simmons.

The next day he set about the task of re-
establishing his grocery business. He looked
up a suitable building, not far from the place
where the old one had stood. His white
friends stood good for him with the wholesale dealers and thus he was enabled to secure a stock that was even larger, and superior to the one which had been lost in the
fire. He also found his trade increasing. The
fire had been a great advertisement for him
and his business. His old friends all came
back to him and brought others with them.
Words of sympathy and good cheer were
everywhere expressed to him. He learned
this lesson that life is a succession of victor-
ies and defeats, that grief and despair are
transitory as are also pleasures and happiness. They all come and go.

CHAPTER XVIII

MRS. SIMMONS VISITS CHARLES

He thought of his weakness the night of the fire and felt ashamed of himself for his tears.

Many of his friends would come in and refer to George Simmons in a way not at all complimentary, but Charles would never discuss that side of the question, and the people could not guess the reason why.

"He will go to the penitentiary sure," some would say to him.

"O, I guess not" or "I hope not," would be his only comment.

Poor Mrs. Simmons was so distressed that she came to see him one day, regarding the coming trial.

She had been reading the papers which seemed to be so bitterly against George, and this together with the view that Frank Maxwell took of the case assuming that her son was guilty really upset her. She did not know which way to turn. And past experiences taught her not to rely too much upon the confidence and security of which Captain

Simmons was often given to boast. So not wishing to leave any stone unturned in the effort to free her son, she hit upon the plan to go and talk to Charles Christopher. She did not know what good might come of it.

One afternoon when there was a lull in his business, Charles Christopher was greatly surprised to see Mrs. Simmons entering his place.

She spoke pleasantly to him and introduced herself as Mrs. Simmons, the mother of George Simmons whom she was quite sure that he knew.

"I wish to talk to you on some business," she said, after the usual preliminaries about the weather, the times and things in general.

"You have no private apartments, have you Mr. Christopher?" she asked.

"No," returned Charles. "Just have a seat back here at my writing desk," said he.

Charles Christopher readily guessed from her last question that she did not wish to be observed in a conversation with him. So in this way with her face behind the high desk she was entirely hid from the passersby or those who might enter for the purpose of trading.

She thanked him for his consideration and made a mental note of his gentility.

Then she began to disclose her reason for coming to him.

She began, "Mr. Christopher, my boy is innocent of the crime with which he is charged." This being her opening attack, she looked Charles squarely in the eye to see how her words would affect him. "And he is being wrongfully held," she proceeded. "'Tis true that he is not in a physical prison, but he is in a mental one, and will continue to be until his innocence is proven. Circumstantial evidence is against him, and public sentiment seems to be against him, but with all that, Mr. Christopher, my boy is innocent. He would not stoop to such a low trick as that. Do you think he would?" Putting the question direct she watched Charles narrowly and waited for him to reply. Charles not wishing to hurt her feelings or to shake the confidence which she had in her son, attempted an evasive answer, but with little success. Not being given to lies and deceit, he said: "Well Mrs. Simmons, guilty or not guilty, I have nothing to do with it. The matter is beyond my control. And you cannot blame me for anything that might happen to George. I have never accused him 'Tis true that we have had our differences, but at the same time, I have always respected him and thought well of him. I am very sorry that this thing happened, and unfortunately for him and the rest of your family he has been charged."

"But you have not answered my question, Mr. Christopher. Do you think he committed the deed?" she asked again.

"Well," returned Charles, attempting to console and at the same time to be frank and truthful, "I think he may expect justice at the hands of the court. It really is not for me to say whether he is innocent or guilty."

"But you can say whether you think him guilty or not," said Mrs. Simmons insistingly.

"Well, Mrs. Simmons, to be frank with you, I am afraid that George is guilty. I think he is a fine fellow, but he is a person who does not want to be overcome. He is always seeking revenge, and this revengeful spirit which is the weakest link in the chain, has been his undoing. I really think that he yielded to a thirst for revenge, and thinking that the deed could be concealed, set fire to the building in which my goods and future prospects lay. I, his enemy as he thought, was prospering and he could not bear the idea of my outstripping him in the race of life. So, to impede my progress, he hits upon this unbecoming method of doing so. But I am quite sure that he has repented and were it to do over again he would not attempt it. But, as I say, it is beyond my control. But if there is anything that I can do to help him or you or any member of your family, Mrs. Simmons, all you have to do is ask it, and you may rest assured that if it is possible for me to do it, I will."

Mrs. Simmons looked at him curiously and finally remarked, "Well, every one seems to be against my boy. I am sorry, indeed, that you think him guilty. If you really think him so, then there is nothing that I can ask of you. The trial will come up soon, now, and I am afraid they may fasten the crime on him. If they do, it will kill me. I can not bear the thoughts of my son going to prison."

"Cheer up, Mrs. Simmons. George has always carried himself properly. He has a good record and I am quite sure that the court will deal with him fairly and leniently, if found guilty. This one overt act is pardonable. He is only human. No doubt he was provoked to such a deed. No one knows the intensity of his feeling at that time. Under passion we so often do and say things that we afterward regret. And if George is guilty, I know that he has repented a hundred times. So be big, broad and brave, Mrs. Simmons, and remember that George is young and without experience, that much older and matured persons have done rash,

reckless and even malicious deeds and have
been excused for them. I hold nothing
against George. I have made excuses for
him, and can overlook the injury that he has
done me. I only wish it were in my power to
have the charge withdrawn."

"You are right, Mr. Christopher. While
I believe my boy innocent, I myself have
twitted him about your success in business
and the humble position which he holds as a
porter. I did it for the purpose of spurring
him on to better things. I should so much
like to see him in business for himself as you
are. His education is of no benefit to him
where he is and he seems to have lost his
ambition and is willing to drudge the rest of
his days. So I have been after him about
being so unconcerned about the future and I
referred to you as an example. He did not
like it very much. But I wanted to arouse
him and make him ashamed of himself. So,
perhaps he has had enough to provoke him;
perhaps my talk did wound his pride, but I
am sure he did not resort to such a foul
method of revenge. You could not help it.
And George, being a sensible boy, would not
blame you, to such an extreme extent, at least.
I want to free him because I believe him
innocent, but I scarcely know what steps to
take. I thank you very much for your

sensible, at the same time, consoling words. I do believe that you are willing to lend your aid, but at present know of nothing that I could ask of you.

"Well, I must be going now. I thought I would come in and see you and get your opinion. I thank you very much for your offer of assistance. I like you, now, since I have met you and know you better. I may come to see you again ere long. Good-day."

"Good-day, Mrs. Simmons," said Charles, "I shall be glad to see you at any time."

Mrs. Simmons departed with a peculiar, but not unpleasant feeling. She thought of the wisdom with which Charles Christopher spoke and of his true delineation of character and of his interpretation of certain unseemly acts. He seemed to be an adept at reading human nature. And when she began to think about it, perhaps he was right in regard to George's motive for burning his store.

Then the thought began to rise within her, that perhaps George was guilty of the crime, but she quickly dismissed it from her mind. She would not or could not realize the possibility of such a thing. Her son was too well bred for such as that. "Low ideas and low minds do not run in the Simmons blood," she said consolingly to herself. "No, no, no," she thought, "George is innocent and we must free him, we must not allow the poor boy to suffer untold agony on account of falsehoods and on account of conspiring unscrupulous enemies.

"But I do have more faith in Charles Christopher, now. I do not believe that he has anything to do with the plot to ruin George. Naturally, though, he would believe George guilty, because George has shown himself to be such an enemy. I always told George to control himself. One never knows from what source he may want and need assistance. I understand that this fellow Christopher has strong influential friends among the people of the other race. He is really in a position to befriend us or to do us great harm. I scarcely think, though, that he would do us an injury. I believe he means to help us if he can. I think I shall cultivate his friendship."

These and other thoughts passed through the mind of Mrs. Simmons rapidly as she trudged homeward.

CHAPTER XIX

A Grave Situation

The day of the trial was fast approaching and every one was looking forward to it. Many were the opinions expressed regarding the chances that George would have to escape punishment. Frank Maxwell still insisted that the best thing to do was for George to plead guilty and ask clemency. He had felt the pulse of those in authority and had learned that it was their intention to inflict the extreme penalty of the law for the offense which George had committed.

He told Captain Simmons that he knew something about the law regarding such offenses, and being a friend of the family he was giving to him, free of charge, the benefit of his best advice based upon experience and practice in former courts. That if they went to trial with the case they were certain to get the worst of it. That George would be sure to go to prison for not less than five years.

This assertion made by Maxwell made Captain Simmons very uneasy and as the

time drew nearer and nearer his nervous-
ness became more and more perceptible. He
was rather obstinate, though, and would not
back down from his determination to fight it
out to the end.

That night at the supper table, when
all three of the family were seated, Captain
Simmons said to George: "Tell me the truth,
son, you did not set fire to Christopher's store,
did you?"

"No, father, I did not," said George.

"Well, son, I am afraid it's going pretty
hard with you. Frank Maxwell says that he
has talked with the authorities and that if
they find you guilty they will send you to the
prison for not less than five years. He thinks
that the best thing you can do is to plead guilty and beg for mercy at the hands of the
court.

"If you were guilty, I guess that would
be the proper thing to do, but since you are
not guilty, we will fight to the bitter end. It
may break us up, but I will gladly give up
everything I have to save you from prison
if you are innocent."

George did not say very much. He sat
trembling. He was afraid to attempt a reply
lest his speech should betray him.

His mother watched him closely and tried to note a change in his countenance or the least sign of guilt in his manner.

But George managed, through great effort, to control himself.

The thought of his father sacrificing the home and everything for him, and he guilty, was killing him.

He would give anything to get out of the scrutinizing gaze of his parents at that moment.

His mother, continuing to watch him, finally said. "George, I can not believe that you are guilty of the crime. It would break my heart to know that you were. I doubt if I could survive the shock. But if you are, as Frank Maxwell says, it will be a whole lot better for you to acknowledge it. Your good record as a citizen and your father's influence will be in your favor. The court will be inclined to be lenient with you. If sentenced, you will have a chance to have it stayed or revoked.

"Besides, if you are guilty, my son, your father and mother are the ones to know it. So, if through weakness or through a thirst for revenge, a desire to play even, you thoughtlessly did the deed, tell us now, George, so we can do the best we can for you."

"I did not do it, mother. I am sorry that

you doubt me. The strain is killing me, I do wish it were all over," said George, sorrowfully.

"Well, right or wrong, George, I am going to stand by you," said his father. "So if you are wrong you need not fear to tell me."

"Well, I never did it," was George's last reply.

After supper was over and George had gone, Mr. and Mrs. Simmons discussed the gravity of the situation. They concluded that since George stood out so stoutly that he was innocent, that they would stay with him to the end, even if it should take the clothes from off their backs.

CHAPTER XX

LILLIAN'S DISTRESS

Lillian received her letter from her mother and Charles Christopher the same day.

She had a real hard day in connection with her school work. The closing season was on and she had been quite busy training the pupils under her supervision. She was real tired that afternoon when she reached home and found the two letters awaiting her.

She was always anxious to get mail from home, so now she was eager to read what they contained.

She hastily tore open the one from her mother and read it first. She was shocked at the news of George's arrest and accusation.

What could it mean? Someone trying to disgrace her brother! She became very indignant, and felt like quitting her work and taking a trip home to see about it at once. After reading it she laid it aside and took the one from Charles Christopher and began reading it.

When she came to the part assuming George's guilt, her heart, it seemed, leaped into her mouth and a choking sensation seized her and overwhelmed her. She was dazed. She staggered from the piano against which she was leaning, and fell across her bed, and for a long time she lay in a sort of silly hysterical stupor. Try as she may, she could not collect herself. Everything was so foolishly blank to her.

She was finally called to supper but she answered that she did not care for anything to eat.

It not being her custom to remain in her room long after returning from school, Mrs. McVain became alarmed about her and went to the room to see if she were ill.

"No, I am not ill," said Lillian, in answer to her question, "I just don't care for supper."

"Did you get your letters?" asked Mrs. McVain. "Two came for you."

"Yes, I received them," answered Lillian. "They contained news that was not very pleasant. That is what's the matter with me, Mrs. McVain. I may tell you about it later. I am trying to collect myself, now."

Lillian lay thus till late at night, when she fell into a deep sleep. The rest and the slumber had its effect. It aroused her to complete consciousness.

She began to think of the letters and the unpleasant, as well as the unfortunate news that they contained. It looked reasonable to her that George might have committed the deed. Charles Christopher's letter was so explicit, so frank, that she scarcely had room to doubt the truth of its contents.

She realized that the love of her mother would cause her to make things as bright as possible for George.

Naturally, her letter contained just what it did, an injured tone, a suspicion that someone was trying to do the family an injury, on account of envy and jealousy.

In other words, her mother's letter was true to human nature, and to a mother or near relative or friend.

She also analyzed Charles Christopher's letter. She noted its friendly attitude. Although it accused her brother, it also contained a tone of sympathy and good will.

She would have appreciated the way in which he referred to Mae Lester under any other conditions, but at this time she was too grieved or too interested in the business of her brother's trial to fully appreciate the tenderness of the letter or of the tendency toward love. The part that suited her most was where he offered to aid her in trouble. This part of the letter greatly impressed her, thought she decided not to reply. One reason was that her school work would soon be over and she would return home, and if she saw fit she could then have a heart to heart talk with him and make explanations.

Besides, she was not quite sure whether she wanted to cultivate Charles Christopher's friendship further, since her family had been disgraced by the low act of her brother. For she was almost convinced that he committed the deed, but before making up her mind to that effect she would have to see him, face to face, and hear his side of the story. She would suspend judgment until then. If George were innocent she might continue with Charles Christopher, but if guilty, she did not know about it. She felt that the embarrassment would be more than she could stand.

The next morning Lillian arose, ate breakfast and made preparations for school. She hastily wrote a letter home to her mother. She did not tell how shocked she was to receive the missive containing the ill news, but instead she tried to cheer her mother.

"My school will soon close, mother, then I will be home and help to secure brother's release," she said. "We can take the money with which we intended to pay off the mortgage and fight the case. I am very anxious

to see you all. And I have much to tell you
of this beautiful Southland. Look for me
next week.

    "Your affectionate daughter,

                "Lillian."

    Thus she concluded her letter and handed
it to an urchin to mail. She then went, with
a mind that was comparatively calm, to her
work. She was resigned and willing to accept whatever might come. Her greatest desire was to finish her term work and get home
as quickly as possible. She knew that her
father and mother must be greatly distressed
and she was anxious to share with them in
their troubles.

    The few days remaining for her work
quickly passed and Lillian found herself at
the station, among many admiring friends
and school children, waiting for the arrival
of the train which was to bear her away
toward her Northern home.

    When the train arrived she bade them all
adieu, and with a promise to return again
another year, she boarded it, found a comfortable seat, and with a sigh of relief sat
down.

    She was the only passenger, at that time,
in the separate coach, and it was such a relief for her to be alone. Resting her head on
the back of her seat she sat for a long time
and felt comfortable.

On her journey she encountered or witnessed only one case of real roughness.

At a certain stop, Lillian did not notice the name of the place, two or three drunken roughs got on the train. They did not say anything to Lillian but they were loud and boisterous, and seemed to be trying to show themselves.

One of them dropped a bottle of whiskey on the floor which broke, spilling its contents, which ran in all directions.

They laughed and yelled to the top of their voices.

Poor Lillian was frightened out of her wits.

One of them gave a yell sharp and piercing as a Comanche Indian. He followed it up with the expression, "come and git me white folks, I'm drunk and cutting up."

He staggered and fell about in the car until the conductor came in and threatened to put him off. The threat had its effect, for all three were quieter. They got off soon and left Lillian to herself once more. After midnight the porter came to her and informed her that she could go in the chair car, now, if she liked, that they had crossed the line and the "Jim Crow" car law no longer obtained.

She thanked him, and he took her baggage and led the way to the beautiful chair

car in which were a number of white passengers.

She noted the contrast and thanked
Heaven that she lived in a country where
such was not the case, and where such was
not necessary.

CHAPTER XXI

_____

LILLIAN AT HOME

Lillian was ~~soon~~ seated and remained comfortable to the end of her journey.

Her mother and father were waiting at the station when she alighted from the train. Placing her in the family carriage, she was soon at home once more, ascending the steps to the broad veranda.

It is useless to speak of the happiness and sunshine that she brought with her. We all know her and love her, especially for her cheerful disposition, her readiness to speak words of consolation to her troubled parents, and her philosophical way of looking at things.

She would not discuss that part of the trouble that pertained to George's innocence or guilt. Though, like her father, she was willing to stick by him to the end. Yes, she would gladly give up every dollar that she had earned and saved from her work in the South, in his behalf. With tears in her eyes she told him so.

George listened to her and seemed so hurt. He was as humble as a child. She could not turn from him. He was so uneasy and seemed to find consolation only in her presence. When he was not at work he was at home following her from room to room. He would plead with her not to worry herself about him. "I'll come out alright," he would say.

But Lillian was not so confident. She could not help worrying, though she had the good sense and enough control to hide her nervous feelings.

She talked mostly of the Southland and told of the great possibilities that it held for the colored race.

Her mother was greatly surprised at some of the things that Lillian told her. A town controlled by colored people was far beyond her ken, and when Lillian Simmons gave such a glowing account of the growth, the prosperity, and the magnificence of the place whence she had so recently returned, her mother thought that she was exaggerating. She could not comprehend the truth of her statements.

Captain Simmons was too busy thinking about and planning for the coming trial, to listen to her never-ending chatter about the sunny Southland.

"Wait, daughter," he would say, "until this trouble is over, and then we will discuss the people of the South.

"The trial comes up Thursday, I am told, and until then we will be very busy.

"We hope George will come out alright, but you can never be too sure.

"These lawyers are mighty sharp these days.

"I need about two hundred dollars more money, have you that much to spare, my dear?"

He asked the question in despondent tones which bespoke much doubt.

"Yes, papa," replied Lillian, "I have four hundred dollars. And you may have it all if you need it."

"Well, daughter, I don't want to break you. Let me have three hundred dollars and when we get kind a straight, I will pay you back or see that George does."

"Papa, that will be alright if you never pay it back. I owe you that and a whole lot more that I can never be able to pay. You have done so much for me and it makes me so happy to know that I can do this much for you. Papa, you seem to be so worried, cheer up. I don't have the least doubt but what George will get out of this trouble. You will worry yourself sick at this rate.

"Come, brace up, for my sake. Wait a moment and I will get the money for you."

Lillian soon returned with the money for her father, for which he thanked her and proceeded on his way to the city.

He paid his lawyers what he had to spare, and then went to see some of his friends regarding the trial, which was to come up in a day or two.

They did not give him much satisfaction, but they told him that they would do the best they could for him.

"You see, Simmons," one of them said, "the charge is a grave one and the evidence is so overwhelmingly against him, that it is going to be difficult to clear him. But you have a good lawyer and I feel quite sure that if anything can be done, he will do it."

CHAPTER XXII

The Trial

The day of the trial had at last come. It was set for nine o'clock. Everything was astir in the Simmons home. The atmosphere was not one of sorrow or grief, but was business-like and comparatively cheerful.

At the breakfast table they chatted pleasantly about the weather and other things of a local nature, never alluding to the trial.

George, himself, seemed in good spirits and joked his sister about Charles Christopher. For by some indiscreet utterance on her part she, to a certain extent, had betrayed her admiration for him.

At his sally she made no denial, but blushing, laughed good-naturedly. Girl-like, she did not mind being teased about the one that she admired.

Her mother never told her of the visit to Charles Christopher's store or the conversation that she had with him, but she did tell her that she had seen him and had spoken to him and liked his manner and appearance very much.

She said she did not much blame Mae Lester for trying to attract his attention; that she thought the two would make a splendid match.

Lillian listened to her mother very closely and was not at all pleased with her view of what she called a splendid match.

"Just wait until this trial is over," she thought. "I'll show Mabel Lester and mother, too, what is really a fine match. They do not know that I have some 'say so' about it."

After finishing breakfast, George and his father departed for the scene of the trial. And Lillian and her mother followed later. When they arrived, the court house was packed to its utmost capacity. The janitor or usher had to go out and find chairs for them, so that they might be seated.

The lawyers, principals and witnesses, were in their appointed places.

On account of the heinousness of the crime, the airing that the papers had given it, and the popularity of the perpetrator, the trial attracted more than ordinary attention.

Hence, white and colored, alike, were interested in the outcome. And Lillian and her mother had to wend their way through a vast gaping, vulgar crowd, which was scenting scandal and gossip.

The hour of nine arrived and the Judge called the court to order.

A jury was empaneled, the charges against George Simmons were read by the clerk, and other things necessary to procedure were over.

Silence reigned for a moment, all were expectant; when the attorney for the state arose and began the examination of witnesses.

"Judge, your honor, may I say a word."

All looked in the direction of the speaker.

It was George Simmons who had thus addressed the court.

"What is it that you wish to say?" inquired the Judge.

"I am not familiar with the methods of procedure in court and I beg pardon, if I am violating rules or in any way interrupting the business in hand, but I desire to make a statement."

"You may proceed, sir," said the Judge.

Captain Simmons moved uneasily and Mrs. Simmons looked aghast. While Lillian leaned forward with increased interest.

George's voice rang out clearly and distinctly. It was accompanied, however, by a slight tremor or quaver, caused mostly by his earnestness of purpose and partly by his being unaccustomed to speak in public.

He began, "Judge, your honor, I deem it unfair and unnecessary to put this court to further trouble or to further expense. I am guilty of the crime for which I am charged."

This sudden confession took the Judge, the jury, and all participants off their feet. The whole house was greatly surprised and strained every nerve to catch what was being said.

George had a natural gift for oratory and his first utterance seemed to electrify him. His keen eyes flashed fire, and his countenance lit up and fairly beamed with emotion. The spiritual man was plainly in the ascendancy.

And George Simmons, for a few moments, held Judge, jury and audience as it were in a spell.

"I am, indeed, sorry that I have for so long kept my father, mother, sister and friends deceived. Here they are, sitting at my back, ready to sacrifice everything in my behalf because they believe in me, because they think me innocent.

"But my conscience will not allow me to deceive them longer. I committed the atrocious deed, because I hated Charles Christopher and did not want to see him prosper. In an hour of weakness, provoked by the chiding which my mother had given me on account of my lack of enterprise, my neglect of opportunity, my seeming indifference to the real purpose of life, I set fire to his store.

"I hated him first because he was a Southerner and because he once came near beating me in a fight. And when my mother twitted me about him and held him up as a shining example for me to follow, I despised him, and thought to ruin him by applying the torch to his prosperous business.

"But, Judge, your honor, I have been sorry a thousand times for the deed. My soul has oft revolted at its atrocity and I have suffered untold agony.

"But a few days ago I carried the matter to a court far superior to this one, Judge, your honor. My case has been tried and settled in the Court of Courts, and I do not rise asking clemency or mercy at your hands, but I rise to satisfy my conscience and to disillusion those of my relatives and friends who have stood so loyally by me.

"A term in prison can not be worse than what I have already suffered.

"So fix the penalty as you will. You and your court are human. You do not understand the workings of the heart like the Judge who has already passed on my case. You could not forgive the offense, and I would not have you change or in any way evade the

"My case has been tried and settled in the
Court of Courts."

law in my behalf. I am willing and able to take the consequences as the law provides.

"I am an awful sinner before you men, but before God I am cleansed and a changed man. I am consoled in this thought.

"I thank you, Judge, your honor, for extending to me this privilege, for I find that an open confession is indeed good for the soul, and I feel much better, now, that I have made it."

George took his seat and the deathly silence that reigned for a few moments afterwards, the appearance of the white handkerchief here and there in audience, and the occasional inelegant blowing of a nose, told that his speech had had its effect.

The Judge sat motionless for a few moments, not knowing what to say or do. He gazed steadfastly at George the while, his fine large head conspicuous for its high brow, and smoothly shaven face with its classical features, wore a puzzled look.

At length, he said, "George Simmons, your crime is a lowdown, unprincipled heinous one, and the penalty for such is not less than five, or more than twenty years at hard labor in the penitentiary, and had you not at this late hour made the plea of guilty, I suspect you would have been given the limit, for such would have surely been my instructions to the jury.

"But your plea has helped you, though irregular and out of order, it is frank, earnest, and, I might say, noble. And in my judgment I do not think it studied or made for effect.

"And I am going to take it upon myself to dismiss the case against you. I think this act of mercy, or clemency, or kindness if you please, on my part will make you a much better man than the penitentiary possibly can. Pay the cost of the court and you are free!"

The Judge spoke slowly and deliberately, and it was quite a relief to the strain on the nerves of the Simmons family, when finally he reached the place where he said that he was going to dismiss the case against George.

George thanked the Judge for his kindness and told him that henceforth a straightforward Christian life was the life for him.

He then went over to Charles Christopher and extended his hand. Charles seized it firmly, and fervently congratulated him on his speech and told him how glad he was to have things turn out as they had.

"Come and meet my folks," said George. "I want them to know you."

Court having been dismissed, Charles followed George to where his mother and

"Come and meet my folks," said George. "I
want them to know you."

sister stood, somewhat embarrassed at George's plea, yet pleased because he had obtained his liberty.

"Mother, this is Mr. Christopher, of whom you have heard so much," said George.

"I am pleased to meet you, Mr. Christopher," returned Mrs. Simmons.

"This is my sister Lillian, Mr. Christopher," said George, presenting Lillian to Charles.

"I am delighted to meet you, Miss Simmons," said Charles in tender accents noticeable only to Lillian, as he grasped her extended hand. The handshake was gentle, but to save her, Lillian could not help giving Charles' hand a little squeeze. She was ashamed, afterwards, when she felt the same returned in her own hand.

The two never pretended that they had met before or that they were in any way acquainted.

Mrs. Simmons also accepted the introduction without saying, "We have met before."

After saying a few words about the weather and the time of day, Mrs. Simmons announced that they must be going.

"Will you walk with us, Mr. Christopher?" she asked.

Without answering, Charles started off with them.

When they reached the door of the court-room Mrs. Simmons and George walked ahead, which proceeding threw Lillian and Charles together.

Captain Simmons was left behind because he was so busy receiving congratulations, and discussing the merits of George's speech. He was proud of him, notwithstanding his guilt. Captain Simmons was always glad to show off in public, and the speech that George made, freeing himself from the clutches of the law more than delighted the old man.

He liked to hear them say, "He's a chip off the old block." So he lingered about town all day, nearly, waiting and listening for such compliments. The party soon reached their gate and Charles Christopher was invited into the Simmons home. He and Lillian entered the parlor.

"Have a seat, Mr. Christopher," said Lillian, pointing to a nearby chair.

Alone, the two seemed to be very much embarrassed, and for a long time they were at a loss to know what to say.

It seemed to Charles that the whole machinery of his brain was out of commission. Try as he may, it would produce no intelligent thought, no befitting words to say to this beautiful young woman whom he loved and in whose presence he now found himself.

At length, after what seemed to be an age of silence, Lillian was the first to speak.

"Well, I am glad that the ordeal is over," she said, as she rocked to and fro in the large chair.

"We have all been so worried, and poor George seemed to suffer so much mental anguish that I was really afraid that he might lose his mind."

"I am glad, too, Miss Lillian, that the great ordeal is over," said Charles, pulling his chair up close to Lillian's side.

Once the awful silence was broken the young man grew bolder.

Lillian never attempted to draw away from him, neither did she show the least sign of displeasure at his act. She smiled faintly, however, and continued to discuss the trial and its outcome.

"I am truly glad that your brother is free," said Charles, "and I am glad to see you and your family restored to happiness again. Would that that happiness could last forever. But happiness is fleeting," he added, as he thought of his own struggles and triumphs.

"Yes, I have always found it so," returned Lillian.

After another brief spell of silence, Charles boldly taking Lillian's hand, said: "I have reasons to believe that you care for me, Miss Simmons."

"I do, indeed," she returned. "You are so kind and manly, one could scarcely keep from caring for you."

"Do you really mean it?" he asked.

"Why, I have always had this opinion of you, Mr. Christopher, do you doubt me?" she asked in an injured tone.

"Well, my dear," he said, putting his arms around her, and drawing her close to him, "you mean it, then this is the brightest day of my life. I am truly the happiest man on earth."

Lillian did not resist him, but lay quite still with her head resting sweetly and trustingly on his heaving breast, murmuring partly to herself and partly to him who now held her so tenderly in his strong arms, "I love you, I love you. I can not hide it, I can not deny it nor do I care to do so."

And thus these two, whom fate had for so long held apart, sat in silent and unspeakable bliss.

Then, planting kiss after kiss upon the lips of the beautiful girl, Charles asked, "Lillian, my love, will you be mine?"

The answer came in accents, sweet and tender. "Yes, Charles, I will. O I am so happy," she cried.

Then the girl, filled with rapture and emotion, gave way to tears.

CHAPTER XXIII

THE CONCLUSION

The title of our story is "Lillian Simmons," or "The Conflict of Sections," and if we make too much of the courtship, love and marriage of Charles Christopher and Lillian Simmons, we will be drifting too far from our main purpose, which chiefly is to call attention to certain social evils and practices nurtured, as it were, by false notions of life and false standards of character or individual worth, and which have a tendency more than anything else to hold us down and impede our progress as a race.

Do you remember old man Littlejohn's speech in the early chapters of this book?

If you have forgotten it, turn to it again and read it over carefully and you will get a clear idea of what we mean by certain social evils and practices and false notions of life.

While we deal with a few of the detriments to the growth and progress of the race, old man Littlejohn, in his unpolished speech, points out several, which are based upon prejudice, and a very narrow conception of the true standards of society.

It is at these things that we are striking. We are trying to unite the North and the South. We are trying to get them to think along the same lines. We would have the North enter more into the spirit of trade and commerce for themselves, and we would have the South develope a higher spirit of manhood and courage to protect itself when outraged. And we would recommend more of the spirit of unity in both sections. The race is woefully lacking in unity in itself both North and South.

Charles Christopher's success in the grocery business, in this Northern city, opened up the eyes of others who had business inclinations, but not the initiative or the confidence in themselves to start. Since his advent several good Negro businesses have been established. Two more grocery stores, one drug store, a cleaning and dyeing and tailor shop, a good restaurant, which caters to both races, a confectionery, and a ladies' clothing and notion store with Mrs. Simmons as proprietress.

Charles Christopher has taken on a partner. The sign now reads, in large letters, "Christopher and Simmons Grocery Store."

Yes, Charles Christopher and George Simmons have not only become great friends, but they have also become brothers-in-law and partners in a very prosperous commercial venture.

A Business League has been organized with Charles Christopher as its president. And such harmony and progress was never before known in this city among the colored people.

Northerners and Southerners view life through the same glass in this city. They are united by the ties of friendship, by ties of business and by the ties of matrimony. It is difficult to break such a combination.

Think of the Simmons family's earlier stand against Southern colored people, and think of their stand now.

They are converted to the idea of Negro enterprise, even if it does invite segregation. They have become convinced that separate schools are not harmful, but are a positive benefit to the race. They furnish employment for the worthy boys and girls of the race and are inducements for them to pursue the higher courses of learning and to strive to excel in them.

Captain Simmons now believes in them, and Frank Maxwell offers no serious objections to them.

Hence, they have a colored school that can not be excelled in efficiency of teaching

United by the ties of business and by the ties
of love.

force, and in equipment anywhere in the country.

Lillian Simmons recommended one of her Southern associates for a position in the school. She is a beautiful Southern girl, from a Southern university. Mrs. Simmons, who used to look upon a Southern College as a joke, and its graduates as ignoramuses, loves her, and admires her for her intelligence and scholarship. The young woman makes her home with Lillian, and George Simmons is a constant caller. It is rumored that there is soon to be another wedding in the Simmons family.

Three years have passed since the day of the trial and George has proven himself worthy of the companionship of any young woman.

The city boasts of one colored dentist and one physician.

Frank Maxwell is no longer custodian of a down town bank building, but has again taken up his profession and practice as a lawyer, and his people are patronizing him. He often lectures to them, and is now advocating the doctrine of unity, and patronage of one's own enterprises.

Six years have passed since that great mass meeting in which so much prejudice and hatred was poured forth in eloquent out-

bursts, in which so many false notions and
ideas were advanced. One could scarcely believe such a radical change could take place
in so short a time. They are all a happier
and a wiser lot now, and Charles Christopher
sees in reality what he pictured the day he
entered the city, in quest of a suitable place
to begin business. The subconscious feeling,
the day dream, and the castle built in the air,
an hour just before entering in the city that
day, have become as truly real for him as
such things often do. Charles Christopher is
a worthy leader of his people, a prosperous
business man and the husband of the beautiful Lillian Simmons. He has not only enabled
the family to pay off their harassing debts,
but he owns his home which was built and
fashioned to Lillian's own taste.

Lillian and Charles think as much of
their baby girl as the "Newly Weds" do of
"Snookums."